Selected Short Stories of
PADRAIC COLUM

Irish Studies

Padraic Colum, age twenty-four. Courtesy of Special Collections, Glenn G. Bartle Library, State University of New York at Binghamton.

Selected Short Stories of
PADRAIC COLUM

edited by
SANFORD STERNLICHT

SYRACUSE UNIVERSITY PRESS   1985

Copyright © 1985 by Syracuse University Press, Syracuse, New York 13244-5160
All Rights Reserved
First paperbound printing 1986

"Eilis: A Woman's Story" and "The Flute Player's Story" from *Studies.* Dublin: MANSEUL,
   1907.
"The Little Pension" from *The Living Age,* May 29, 1909.
"Marriage," "Land Hunger," "The Slopes of Tara," and "Marcus of Clooney" from *Road
   Round Ireland.* New York: MACMILLAN, 1926. Reprinted with permission of
   Macmillan Publishing Company. Copyright 1926 by Macmillan Publishing Co.,
   Inc., renewed 1954 by Padraic Colum.
Three Men. London: ELKIN MATTHEWS & MARROT, 1930.
"Catherine Mulamphy and the Man from the North" and "The Death of the Rich Man"
   from *Cross Roads in Ireland.* New York: MACMILLAN, 1930.
"The Peacocks of Baron's Hall" from *Catholic World,* May 1933.
"A Dublin Day" from *Catholic World,* October 1933.
"Pilgrimage Home" from *Catholic World,* March 1945.

Library of Congress Cataloging-in-Publication Data

Colum, Padraic, 1881–1972.
   Selected short stories of Padraic Colum.

   (Irish studies)
   Contents: Eilis, a woman's story—The flute
player's story—Marriage—[etc.]
   I. Sternlicht, Sanford V. II. Title. III. Series:
Irish studies (Syracuse University Press)
[PR6005.038A6   1986]   823'.912   86-14481
ISBN 0-8156-0202-2 (pbk.)

SANFORD STERNLICHT is a poet, critic, historian, and theatre director. His books
include *Gull's Way* (poetry), 1961; *Love in Pompeii* (poetry), 1967; *John Webster's
Imagery and the Webster Canon* (1972); *John Masefield* (1977); *C. S. Forester* (1981);
and *Padraic Colum* (1985). He is also the author of four books on American naval
history of which *McKinley's Bulldog: The Battleship Oregon* (1977) was a Military
Book Club and Saturday Evening Post Book Club selection. Professor Sternlicht
teaches in the English Department of Syracuse University.

Manufactured in the United States of America

CONTENTS

INTRODUCTION

ALTHOUGH PADRAIC COLUM (1881–1972) is best known as a poet, dramatist, and writer of children's literature, he wrote short stories for more than sixty years. They appeared in the early days of *The United Irishman* just after the turn of the century, when young Colum was a leader in the Irish Literary Revival, and they appeared in *The New Yorker* in the 1960s. He helped found the Irish National Theatre Society and the Abbey Theatre, along with William Butler Yeats, Lady Gregory, George Moore, AE (George Russell), and John Millington Synge. Colum feuded with Yeats and others over the subject matter of the new Irish drama and the goals of the Abbey Theatre. That conflict, coming at the time that he left his indelible mark on the Irish stage with his three masterful peasant plays *Broken Soil* (1903, later rewritten as *The Fiddler's House*), *The Land* (1905), and *Thomas Muskerry* (1910), and also coinciding with his growing interest and ability in lyric poetry, as well as with the difficulty of earning a living by belletristic activities in Dublin, caused Colum to leave the Abbey and then to leave Ireland for the economic opportunities in America.

Thus Colum became a "typical" Irish writer of his time: that is, he did not live in Ireland and he hardly wrote about anything but Ireland. His exile was voluntary and it was necessary. Ironically because of his exile Colum kept a vision of "Old" Ireland, town and country, in his head and heart long after that reality had passed from the Irish scene.

In New York Colum was unable to succeed on Broadway. Instead, he perfected his lyric poetry, and he developed a reputation as a folklorist after receiving a commission from the legislature of Hawaii to record the legends of the Islands, which resulted in the publication of *At the Gateways of the Day* (1924) and *The Bright Islands* (1925). Also he wrote biographies of his friends James Joyce and Arthur Griffith, the first president of the Irish Free State; he published two epic novels, *Castle Conquer* (1923) and *The Flying Swans* (1957); and he earned a literary livelihood as the author of more than twenty-five books for young people.

Storytelling for the young gave Colum the opportunity to relive his own childhood in rural Ireland. Indeed, he began to learn the storyteller's craft as an Irish child sitting by a peat fire and listening to adults spin yarns. However, most of Colum's stories for young people are based on folklore and mythology, not on late nineteenth-century Irish peasant life. In gifting the young with his storytelling skills Colum chose to serve as a translator of cultural history: Irish, European in general, Ancient Greek, and even Hawaiian. Also, Colum, having caught the attention of the young through the popularity of his children's books, seized the opportunity to pass on the moral values of the past to future generations. Several of his books for the young are still in print and they have been re-illustrated by contemporary artists.

However, Colum's intentions as a writer of stories for adult audiences were quite different from those he had for his children's stories. His "serious" short fiction, especially those pieces set in Ireland, was to be a part of his prose effort to evoke and in a paradoxical humble way, to exalt the besieged culture and impoverished country of his youth. Colum saw his prose work, particularly in his two novels, as the big gun in his battle with cultural entropy.

Colum's novels were neither great critical successes nor popular triumphs. *Castle Conquer* (1923), an idyllic, poetic romance set in the 1870–80 period of Irish history, depicts the struggle of honest, hardworking peasants to overcome the power of grinding landlords, forever gauging exorbitant rents from the poor. It effectively portrays the panorama of the Irish countryside: the beautiful landscape, the dirty beggars, the grasping shopkeepers, the constabulary, the storytellers, the overworked farmers, and the young people striving to make a decent life for themselves. *Castle Conquer* was just moderately well received, but Colum began to work on a grand scheme to write a three-volume epic novel of nineteeth-century and early twentieth-century Irish life, a *Bildungsroman* recounting the life of a fictional sculptor, Ulick O'Rehill, from birth onwards. Unfortunately, Colum worked too long on the novel, choosing to deal with it as his friend Joyce had dealt with *Finnegans Wake,* treating it as a work in progress and publishing several sections as stories in *The Dial.* The first and only volume of the trilogy, *The Flying Swans,* appeared in 1957. Although it is 538 pages long, it takes the hero only from childhood to young manhood. The critics were indifferent. Colum was primarily a poet and a children's writer to them. They did not give proper, serious attention to the novel, which is Colum's *Ulysses* (Ulick is Gaelic for Ulysses) and which is a grand memorial to and memory of Old Ireland. Disappointed, he gave up his epic and abandoned the novel form.

Padraic Colum's interest in the short story preceded and then accompanied his interest in the novel. He published more than thirty stories for adults. They may be divided into four categories: turn of the century Irish country life, turn of the century Dublin life, Hawaiian stories, and contemporary stories. His best short-story writing by far is in the first two categories, and the thirteen stories in this anthology are those that most finely represent his contribution to the genre, to literature in the English language, and to the cause of the preservation of Irish culture.

Padraic Colum and his wife, Mary Maguire Colum, a noted critic, enjoyed a happy married life for forty-five years, until her death in 1957. They often wrote, lectured, taught, and traveled together. In their old age they came to be revered as the last survivors of the Dublin of the Literary Revival, the age of Yeats and Joyce. But although Padraic Colum walked with giants, and their long shadows tended to obscure him, he was a major figure in the Irish Renaissance, and he made a significant contribution to the new literature of an ancient people rediscovering and redefining their culture in the light of a great, successful political struggle for freedom.

Padraic Colum lived ninety years. He was born at Collumkille, County Langford, Ireland, on December 8, 1881, as Patrick Collumb, first born of eight children of Patrick Collumb, heavy drinker and future emigrant to America; and Susan MacCormack Collumb, daughter of a gardener, who would die, worn out, shortly after the birth of her last child.

Colum had only eight years of formal education. His first employment was as a railroad clerk in Dublin. In 1901 he joined the Gaelic League and the Irish Republican Army. Also, that year he Gaelicized his name to Padraic Colum and began to write poems, stories, and plays. By 1903 he was a leading playwright in Yeats's Irish National Dramatic Company, and the next year he gave up his job to devote the rest of his life to writing. Slowly he changed from a strikingly handsome wisp of a youth to a portly old leprechaun with a red face and a huge, bald Falstaffian head fringed with a white crown. He grew hard of hearing and, as a result, in his sixties he talked much, listened little, and laughed a lot. The blue eyes ever twinkled. At his death on January 11, 1972, in Enfield, Connecticut, after fifty-seven years in exile, he was still an Irish writer.

Colum saw his literary mission as that of Celtic Bard, an itinerant singer of old, who through the lyric, narrative, and dramatic forms evoked and celebrated a time, a place, and a people, using a beloved language with clarity, simplicity, and beauty.

Although writing short stories was a sideline for Colum, storytelling in verse and prose was central to his creative efforts. He often wrote of his debt to the storytellers of his youth.

Colum liked to remind his readers and lecture audiences that he was born in the workhouse of Longford, Ireland, where his father was the master, and that among his earliest memories was the recollection of listening to stories told to him by indigent, landless peasants and tinkers.

Writing just before he died, Colum recalled the influence of his maternal grandmother on his development as a storyteller:

> I spent some years in my grandmother's house in County Cavan. It was not Irish-speaking, but, at the time it was as close to the old life as any English-speaking locality could be. My grandmother often told traditional stories: she had a beautiful one that I never found in any collection, and that I made into a narrative poem. It had an imaginative phrase that I long remembered, "As wise as the man who never told his dream." But she did not tell the stories in any professional way. But there was an old man who came to the house, to the celidh, who was a shanachie, the story-teller and the local historian. I learned about local history by listening to exchanges between him and my grandmother. And in his very dilapidated house—he was afterwards evicted from it, and I now wonder why his neighbours allowed it to be done—by the light of the bog-deal on his fire, I heard him tell stories to the boys and girls who had come in. He remained seated on the bench by the fire as he told the story, a stick in his hand that he raised to emphasize the salient parts of narrative, the runs or repetitions said rhythmically. It stayed in my mind as a performance. Afterwards when I came to write books that were based on legends, this method of oral delivery was in my mind.[1]

Colum's frequent use of a narrator in his short stories dealing with peasant or country life seems to have been derived from these early listening experiences. In some ways the

1. Padraic Colum, "Vagrant Voices: A Self Portrait," *The Journal of Irish Literature* 2 (January 1973): 65.

format of many of Colum's early Irish stories is like that of a one-act play with a simple cottage setting and a narrator observing and commenting on a poignant or humorous scene. Colum's first dramas, both one-act and full-length plays, stem from the same childhood listening experiences as did his stories and narrative poems.

Elsewhere and often, Colum liked to remember his storytelling and musical uncle, Mickey Burns, an itinerant buyer of poultry from the peasants for resale in the town markets. Burns often took his young nephew along on his tours of the countryside:

> We would travel in the fowl-buyer's van. Mickie would pour out an unending discourse about some "bastard" who lived in a house with white pillars before the gate. To my uncle-in-law, any man who was not counted among the adherents of some association he favored was a "bastard." Then for another mile of the road his story would be about the escape of some man wanted by the government, and after that, maybe, about the wild geese coming down to the Bog of Allen. He had the faculty of making all these things seem out of an epic.[2]

After moving to Dublin at the age of seventeen to work as a clerk in a railway office, Colum began a five-year regimen of serious reading, concentrating on Irish literature, Irish history, and European drama. He also undertook a course of study in Gaelic. At this time William Butler Yeats was publishing his Red Hanrahan stories (1897), and in the process legitimizing the folk tale and also, when revised (1904, 1907), making simple peasant speech a part of Irish literature. George Moore's masterpiece novel *Esther Waters* (1894), seemingly as much related to French realism as to the Victorian English novel, had appeared, and then his collection of short stories, *The Untilled*

2. Padraic Colum, "In Pilver Park There Walks a Deer," *New Yorker,* May 31, 1969, p. 35.

Field (1903), encouraged younger Irish authors to write about contemporary Irish situations in a clear, direct English prose. Finally, John Millington Synge, Colum's closest friend and fellow playwright at the Abbey, was incorporating the imaginative life and language of the West Country peasantry into both story and play. With Yeats, Synge, Lady Gregory, and Douglas Hyde available to talk to, and with the first stories of the new Irish fiction at his finger tips, it is not surprising that Colum's early stories as well as plays were set in the countryside with peasant characters of human proportions speaking Irish English and confronting contemporary problems such as the desire for full political freedom, the need to alleviate poverty, and both the revering and the casting off of the past.

Additionally, Colum greatly admired the realistic dramas of Henrik Ibsen and hoped to lead Irish drama away from Symbolist plays and folklore themes to Ibsen-like discussions of Irish moral, emotional, and political problems. His study of Ibsen not only affected Colum's dramaturgy, but also greatly influenced his efforts in short fiction.

In 1906 Colum published an article on Ibsen in which he stated: "There is in Ireland a great feeling for character, not character as the modern novelists conceive it, mere psychological material, but for character living, breathing, moving—in a word acting. There is too a real aptitude for dialogue; newspapers and drawing-room conversation have not taken colour out of speech made by peasants and workpeople."[3]

Colum saw the embracing of Ibsen's values as more than a way to bring realism to Irish literature. Ibsen was to be the model for Irish authors like Colum, writing drama and fiction, in which they would find inspiration and guidance for their efforts to destroy the stage Irishman and the banal peasant jester of so-called Irish humor, and replace them with a genuine Irish character, sometimes serious, sometimes humorous, but always a real person drawn from the countryside or the

3. Ibsen and National Drama," *Sinn Fein,* June 2, 1906, p. 2.

city slums, and always speaking authentic Irish-English. As a playwright Padraic Colum succeeded in this task for fewer than ten years; as a short-story writer he succeeded for more than sixty.

Padraic Colum was a life-long friend of James Joyce. Although they were the same age, Colum, the railway clerk, first secretly admired the university student who as a youth was already building a reputation as both an eccentric and a literateur. Colum soon obtained an introduction and cultivated the friendship which Joyce reciprocated. Colum took his work to Joyce for criticism and he tried to help Joyce in his difficulties in getting his story collection, *Dubliners* (1914), published.

Colum read *Dubliners* nearly ten years before those stories were finally published, and the reader can now see the influence of Joyce's pessimistic view of Dublin life in Colum's longest story, "Three Men," and in the shorter work, "Dublin Day." Also, "Eilis: A Woman's Story" reminds the reader of two of Joyce's stories: "Eveline," in that it presents a girl who cannot cross a ditch that separates her from the man she loves; and "The Dead," when Gretta recalls her dead lover, Michael Fury. In fact, the name of the good but boring middle-class man Eilis finally marries, Michael Conroy, seems to be a combination of Michael Fury and Gretta's husband, Gabriel Conroy.

Padraic Colum made no attempt to edit, collect, and anthologize his short stories after *Studies* in 1907, which contains only two stories—"Eilis: A Woman's Story" and "The Flute Player's Story"—along with the verse drama, "The Miracle of the Corn." He did not neglect the form. He did come to believe that his reputation as an Irish man of letters would be better furthered by reworking his poetry as he did year after year, and finally by attempting the novel. Thus not only did he fail to edit stories which had seen print in American, Irish, British periodicals, but he also left his plays uncollected at the time of his death in 1972.

Colum's best short prose are his stories of the Irish countryside and stories about Dublin. In both cases his style is similar although his purposes are different, for his Dublin stories strongly satirize that city's intellectual and artistic life, while the countryside pieces generally present rural life as dignified, meaningful, and gracious.

These two categories of stories provide the finest examples of Colum's short fiction for two reasons: first, he is on familiar ground with them and he is able to use his excellent ear for dialogue and keen eye for setting to best advantage when writing about the milieu and the events of his youth and early manhood; secondly, these stories are labors of love, especially the peasant stories, for Colum sketched familiar characters and scenes in words obviously stroked onto paper with affection and reverence.

Stylistically, Colum prefers direct declarative sentences, preferably simple or compound rather than complex. He favors the present tense, usually with a third-person narration. Sometimes, as in "Eilis: A Woman's Story." "The Flute Player's Story," and "Marcus of Clooney," Colum double frames his stories by having the narrator hear the story from a participant who is recollecting the events of a tale. Colum generally uses literal rather than figurative imagery except when he is quoting or creating peasant Irish English speech. However, he never uses stage Irish; his Irish English is always credible. Dialogue consists of short, realistic exchanges, with country folk often using a syntax derived from the influence of Gaelic.

Colum takes special care in his descriptions of the Irish countryside. Even though many of his stories were written in America, the author had the ability to sketch the people and the land of Ireland at the turn of the century with a verisimilitude that causes the reader to believe that Colum is walking with him or her across a bog, down a country lane, or through the back streets of a dusty village.

The author uses symbols precisely and sparingly. A favorite is the bird, sometimes representing freedom, sometimes loss or death or gloom, as with scavengers, and sometimes representing artistic and imaginative flight. It is no coincidence that Colum's second and longest novel, one concerning the development of an artist, is titled, *The Flying Swans.*

In the stories collected here peacocks symbolize the lost way of life of the old Irish Catholic aristocracy, a life of gentility, grace, and beauty cursed only by the ineffectualness of those who inherited it and lost it. This is best seen in "The Peacocks of Baron's Hall."

Near the end of his long life Colum remembered being taken as a child by his mother to see an abandoned mansion where peacocks still roamed the ruins:

> My mother beckoned me to a place outside. And there, for the first time, I looked on the magnificence of peacocks. The sight of this parade must have greatly impressed me, for the memory of it is in two, maybe three books I have written. A long time afterward, I was told by the successor of the caretaker my mother knew that the peafowl in that dismantled place were kept there because of an old lease—and what an excellent clause to have in a lease! When I saw them later on—it must have been about twenty years after I had watched them with my mother—they had become wild fowl, roosting on trees and in hayricks, and subject to raids of foxes: the young ones, likely.
>
> Well, here they were, with their azure breasts and crested heads and great trains, coming across what was once the lawn—a great sight for an imaginative six-year-old—their modest peahens beside them: the unforgettable survivals of a mansion's life.[4]

Ravens also live in the ruins of the past as in "The Slopes of Tara." Brendan, the young artist hero of "Pilgrimage Home," a character reminiscent of Ulick, the protagonist of *The Flying Swans,* has birds accompanying him on his quest to find the purpose of his life. On the road: "It was twilight. All the noise that came to him was the gabble of distant geese, the twitter of small birds, the noise of little streams, or, now and

4. "In Pilver Park There Walks A Deer," p. 37.

again, the startled cry of a black bird." At the end of his pilgrimage "the cawing of rooks" awaits him along with other
salutary sounds such as the ringing of a chapel bell, the bellow-
ing of a bull, and the sound of a sledge on an anvil. John
Greggins, in "The Little Pension," unfortunately "lived in
place where the very crows were lonely." The sadder tale, "The
Slopes of Tara," begins with "A young crow perched on a
branch outside, barked insistently into a human habitation."

The absence of bird sound signifies the absence of nature
and beauty in Colum's work. When Mortimer O'Looney, the
poetaster protagonist of "A Dublin Day," who is on his way to
sell his grandmother's extra grave, climbs Nelson's Tower in
Dublin, he finds that: "Of course no lark sang above the city,
and the song of the caged lark could not reach him up here.
But he heard a lark's song. He heard it in his mind's ear." That
is not good enough for a poet and that is why O'Looney is a
bad one; his source and inspiration are ersatz. Perhaps, too, he
is a loon, a fish-eating bird who is helpless on land and who
looks very funny walking.

There is a striking bird image in "The Death of the Rich
Man," Colum's parable about the coming of death to a wealthy
Gombeen man, a peasant dealer who squeezes the poor. A
shuler, that is to say a female tramp, while faking mourning,
waits in the house to steal a couple of empty bottles worth a
penny or two. Colum says: "She stood there like an old carrion
bird. Her eyes were keen with greed and her outstretched
hand was shaking." If not Death itself, the shuler is Death's
companion.

Generally, however, Colum makes no moral judgments.
He lets his characters speak for themselves and justify their
own actions. In the haunting "Flute Player's Story" the reader
is permitted to see the broken-down musician as he envisioned
himself in better days, to weigh the widow's motivation in
rejecting him for a more handsome fellow, and to realize that
love may lead to disastrous choices. Regardless, Colum implies
through his characterization of the flute player, the widow, and

Antinous, her second husband, that each life must come to shabbiness, old age, and a world turned cold. The good choice and the bad choice wind up as the same choice, and in the end we are our illusions.

A major theme in the stories of Padraic Colum is the inherent dignity and nobility of the Irish peasant. Eilis is a graceful and charming peasant woman of eighty. Colum notes: "Generally the older women in this part of the country have the manner that comes from a fine tradition; they have, too, the repose that comes with age, the acceptance, the trust." In "Marriage" Ellen struggles for happiness with a fierce peasant courage that enables her to accumulate the dowry necessary to bring her the husband of her choice.

The peasant activist in "Land Hunger," Michael Heffernan, gives up an easier and more affluent life in England to work the soil of his native land. "To this child of the earth to plough with horses was poetry and ritual." No peasant, even if the character is a comic one, is treated without dignity. Only John Greggins, the British Army pensioner in "The Little Pension" is presented with some derision, presumably because he left his country to serve the occupying power. Serving the British seems to be the one unforgivable sin in Colum's work. His first published play, *The Saxon Shillin'*, is about the subject, truly a hard one for the author to deal with, as his brother, Fred, was a British soldier. Again and again, in story, novel, play, and poem, Colum cries out against what he considered to be mercenary service with the occupying power.

From childhood on, Padraic Colum was enamored of the lyricism and rhythm of the Irish English dialects of the countryside, a language free from literary associations, with Gaelic syntax, metaphor, and vocabulary items. He incorporates Irish English patterns and expressions into his stories whenever possible. Eilis remembers her husband as "A man that wouldn't let me break a sod of turf across my knee, he took such care of me." Admiring the flute player's ability, the narrator exclaims: " 'It's well for you that has the music,' I said to him in Irish." Ellen "swore by the beam of her father's roof that she would leave that house triumphantly, and marry Hugh Daly." In "Land Hunger," "Michael had nature for the land, as they say." When the ballad singer in "The Little Pension" rises to leave, he says, "I must be shortening my road now, ma'am." Again and again Colum makes effective use of dialect and on occasion he salts his stories with actual Gaelic expressions.

The permanence of the Celtic Bard, a singer and story teller, is another of the continuing themes in Colum's stories. In the early stories such as "Eilis: A Woman's Story," "The Flute Players Story," and "Marcus of Clooney," the narrator persona, perhaps representing young Colum himself, is, like an ancient bard, a collector of other people's tales for transmission to future generations. In "The Little Pension" a ballad-singer accompanies John Greggins part of the way to collect the old soldier's pension, singing of County Mayo in Gaelic. In "The Slopes of Tara" the entire story is a folk tale of the modern instance in which a young man dreams of the past glories of his country. He meets a beautiful girl and he knows that back in the ancient time of Irish kings she was his love. Clearly, Colum believes that the oral tradition of Irish culture is an unbroken one from the medieval era to his own and beyond.

Another major theme in Colum's stories is the love of the Irish people for their land, their cultural tradition, and their history. The author is very proud of the fact that the Irish remained a distinct people with their own language, religion, and way of life despite both the long British occupation and the homogenizing influences of the modern world.

In "Marriage" Colum depicts with reverence the difficult but necessary business of arranging marriages for children. Each character plays his or her role according to the ancient customs of a people of the land. When Ellen reaches marriage age she is said to have "the look which a Connachtman saw in the women of the Midlands, *Uisgue faoi thalamh*, 'Water under the ground.' This young girl with her copper-coloured hair and shrewed eyes could hold her own in a game of intrigue." Even when the courting game is treated humorously as in "Marcus of Clooney," it remains intrenched in custom and tradition, and beneath all activities is the serious matter of regenerating a people while continuing their beleaguered way of life.

The peasant farmer, Michael Heffernan, has so great a hunger for a piece of the soil of his native land to farm and to call his own and to pass on to his son that he is willing to risk imprisonment to obtain it. Only after he has land can he look to his son's marriage and the continuance of his race. Also, in "The Slopes of Tara" Shaun dreams an archetypal dream of ancestral participation in the golden age of the early medieval Irish kings, and his dream contrasts sharply with his mean, loveless, subsistence-level life. Colum indicates that the distant past in Ireland was a glorious time, and he implies a hope that post-independence Irish life in the far future may be better.

With as much fervor as he extolls the dignified, honest, intelligent ways of the Irish peasantry, so Colum derides the pretentions of the pseudo-intellectuals, poetasters, and impotent critics of Dublin. As a young man fresh from the country and without much formal education, Colum stood in awe of the intelligentsia and literati he met in Dublin, but that awe was tinged with jealously, and later he would come to believe that Dublin was only a provincial capital in the English-speaking world and that its establishment was hostile to him. His difficulty in earning a living through writing in Dublin would reinforce that view.

In "A Dublin Day" he makes gentle fun of a minor, minor poet named O'Looney, who writes verse for a Sunday edition of a daily newspaper, and who reads papers at meetings of literary societies. Living on a small pension from the days when he was a paymaster to the King's Fifes and Kettledrums, his existence is as lifeless as his clothes, which from "a peg at the back of the room door, hung like a strangled man." He and his fellow poet, Anthony Wade, are badly educated, terribly provincial, and full of self-importance. Colum sees literary Dublin in the 1930s and 1940s as a second-rate place. By implication the best of writers (Joyce and Colum) are in exile. The standards of criticism are even lower.

In *Three Men* Colum attacks more pseudo-intellectuals, minor critics, and narrow-minded scholars. They confer status upon each other, and they join societies such as the imaginary Eblana Literary Society (probably based on Colum's friend Arthur Griffith's Eblana Debating Society) the founder of which is in fact a street photographer of tourists. These unworthies read long, obtuse papers to each other and battle over them. Academic pretension is thoroughly worked over in this satire.

Concurrently, Colum points out in both "A Dublin Day" and "Three Men" that besides the provincialism, the narrowness, and self-serving aspects of Dublin intellectual life, existence in Dublin is also a materially impoverished one. There is simply no way to earn a living directly through belletristic activities, and those critics and writers who remain in Dublin are sentenced to lives of poverty which prevent them from devoting full time to their scholarship, from buying books, and from traveling.

Padraic Colum was an Irish nationalist. His first published poems appeared in Arthur Griffith's *United Irishman* and *The Irish Independent* at the turn of the century. His work as a playwright began when Griffith sponsored him as a member of the Irish literary society called *Cumann na nGaedeal.* The society offered a prize for a play that would speak out against Irishmen enlisting in the British Army. Colum won the prize with *The Saxon Shillin'* and his playwriting career was launched. At an early age he joined the Sinn Fein party and in 1913 the Irish Volunteers. He drilled under arms and helped smuggle guns into the country. In America from 1914 on, he devoted much of his time to raising money for Irish Independence. Naturally, Irish nationalism is a recurring theme in his stories written both before and after the establishment of the Free State.

In "Eilis: A Woman's Story" the old woman laments that she has lost most of her Gaelic: "Acushla, it's a long time since I spoke the Gaelic. The words are like the words of my old songs; I can hardly bring them to mind." The narrator remembers her brother, for her family "was connected with that culture which the country people still hold, fragments of some long descended civilization." Furthermore Eilis' brother was "a good representative of this peasant culture. He lived at the time when the peasants were making an entry into affairs. A nation had been born in the shadow of past defeats and was beginning to stir. As yet the struggle was for a little security, a little knowledge, a little toleration. The tenant farmers of Ireland were closing up for the bitter struggles against feudal privilege; they had not enough detachment to realize the nation."

Colum expresses his anti-British feeling in "The Little Pension." It is ironic that John Greggins, the British Army pensioner who has spent so much time in the foreign service of the occupying power that he does not know his native land, sends an obsequious letter of thanks to the British Government for his small pension just before the authorities arrest him for disorderly conduct of which he is innocent. In "Pilgrimage Home" Brendan's brave soldier friend, Tibbot Burke, "would drill young men in the hope that later on arms could be procured for them. 'These people have never seen their own sort carrying arms. We have come to accept the fact that we are a disarmed population. I want to show the people companies drilling.' "

Since "Pilgrimage Home" seems to take place at the end of the nineteenth century, Colum is indicating the beginnings of the Irish Volunteers and the Irish Republican Army. Brendan's pilgrimage is one not only to find himself and to begin his career as a sculptor, but also to find the Ireland of the future, a free nation that would appreciate the monuments he would sculpt for it.

Colum had few illusions about the Ireland of the future. He fully realized that his native land would still have to struggle against poverty and ignorance long after freedom was won. However, he felt strongly that the Irish people needed to remember and be proud of their recent past. He wanted his readers in Ireland and America to know and appreciate the long struggle of the Irish nation against imperial power and internal ennui. For Colum the best way to achieve this end was to show the quiet, daily courage of those who lived on the land and endured and survived every evil and calamity that came to them down the endless road of their history.

As to Ireland's distant past, the era of the medieval kings, Colum surely had fewer illusions than Yeats or AE. Although Colum romanticized the Heroic Era in his stories and poems, he did not foresee a return to the ways of ancient Ireland as a solution to the problems of the modern nation, nor did he expect a second coming of greatness to lift the Irish people onto the world's stage as a harbinger of a great cultural and moral revival. It would be enough for the Irish people to remember and preserve the best of the past as they made the most of the future. In that way their sufferings and their achievements would not have been in vain, and in a small, but jewel-like way they would be a light unto the nations.

In a less serious vein, Colum enjoys writing about the bellicosity in the Irish character. In "Marriage," for example, Ellen enjoys the contest with her sister-in-law, and when she has won she still continues the battle. Her teasing of her nephew reminds the narrator of an old tale: "The Little Brawl of Allen." In it the hero Finn says: "Well thanks be to God, . . . we are all at peace. It's a long time since we were at peace before. Indeed, we weren't at peace, Goll, since the day I killed your father."

Martin Mulamphy takes on Neil MacNeere, the man from the North in "Catherine Mulamphy and the Man from the North," thinking he is fighting to keep his wife from a seducer only to find out that she was not at all interested in another man, but had thrown away her wedding ring when the "gold" band Martin had bought her five years ago proved to be brass. Fortunately Northerner and Southerner suffer only a few bruises.

In "Catherine Mulamphy and the Man from the North" Colum, in his usual gentle way, is suggesting that the rivalry between Northern Ireland and the Republic of Ireland is a matter of mistaken intentions and of suspicions built on false premises. He also implies a hope that the "misunderstanding" will be resolved with a minimum of pain and hatred. Although his position proved to be Pollyanna-ish, it in no way detracts from the charm and effectiveness of the story.

In "The Little Pension" poor John Greggins, at peace with the world and so grateful to the British Government for his military pension which has just come in the mail, meets some idlers on a bridge. He makes a friendly remark and is greeted with derision. Being an Irishman, he answers mocking words with a blow and the ensuing donnybrook ruins his day to say the least. He is carted off by the police.

No one is ever seriously hurt in Colum's brawls. Fighting, both physical and verbal, lets off steam, and sometimes results in a primitive but effective justice. Colum does not applaud or condemn it; he merely accepts it. Perhaps it can be said that when it comes to fighting, Colum is an interested spectator.

The short stories of Padraic Colum received almost no critical attention during their author's lifetime. Early in Colum's career the critics considered him almost exclusively as a dramatist and they thought of his stories, travel pieces, and general articles as journalistic work written to earn some money in a poor-paying profession. Indeed Colum spoke of himself as a playwright long after his dramas ceased to be performed. After the success of his first book of poetry, *Wild Earth* (1907), and the follow-up success of *Dramatic Legends* (1922) in America, Colum was perceived as an Irish poet, and that categorizing remained unchanged until the author's death. It was tempered only by the attention given to Colum's work in children's literature and folklore. Thus, this book is the first attempt to bring a significant selection of Colum's short fiction to the general reader and, also, to offer an appreciation of this aspect of his work.

Padraic Colum's short fiction is a part of the mainstream of the Irish short story. Primarily it deals with Irish subjects both past and present. It presents the Irish character lovingly but with warts. It is a part of the movement to Realism that swept European literature late in the nineteenth century and which continues in Ireland and elsewhere to this day. Colum's special contributions to Irish fiction include his power to evoke the time and the place of rural Ireland at the end of the nineteenth century and the beginning of the twentieth century, his ability to portray the Irish peasant with dignity and nobility despite the poverty and political deprivation they endured, and his skill in capturing the subleties, nuances, lyricism, strength, and charm of Irish English.

At this writing no story of Padraic Colum is in print anywhere. Except for *Studies* (1907), containing only two pieces of fiction, no anthology of the short stories of Padraic Colum has ever been published until this one. These thirteen stories are not only representative of Colum's storytelling art but, also, they are especially fine examples of the best short fiction produced by the Irish Literary Renaissance. They are a small treasure of Irish culture and a part of Irish history. But most of all, they deserve returning to the light of day because of their intrinsic worth. They offer fine characterization, significant themes, subtle pathos, gentle humor, and deep thought. And, of course, they are a delight to read.

Padraic Colum came from the soil. He was a countryman and a Catholic. Almost none of the major Irish writers of his generation were both. Perhaps because of this his contribution is unique. To the end of his life, long, long after his wife, all his friends like James Joyce, Ezra Pound, Robert Frost, Edward Arlington Robinson, Elinor Wiley, and Van Wyck Brooks had died, Colum remained a storyteller and conversationalist. As he approached his ninetieth year he was still addressing college groups, offering reminiscences about his more famous literary friends, reciting stories and events from the nineteenth century, culling long poems from his memory and delivering them with gusto in his inimitable Irish brogue, and whispering jokes into the ears of pretty coeds. He was a happy man who loved the life he had lived, and who enjoyed sharing what he had known and learned. These selected stories are a significant part of his gift.

Syracuse, New York   SANFORD STERNLICHT
Summer 1984

Selected Short Stories of
PADRAIC COLUM

THE COUNTRYSIDE

EILIS
A Woman's Story

I FOUND EILIS in my aunt's house one autumn evening, and she told me this story. Eilis was knitting stockings for the household. She arose and welcomed me when I came in, and I shook hands with her without realising who the woman was.

My aunt was baking bread for the men who were coming in from the fields, and I went over to where she was at the fire. "Had you any luck with your fishing?" my aunt asked me.

"None at all," I said, "and your man will think less of me than ever now."

My aunt spoke to the woman knitting. "Myles says that the student here has too much dead knowledge to be any good," she said.

"Your man never thought much of them that are fond of books," the woman replied.

"You ought to give Eilis a book," my aunt said to me; "she is very fond of reading." I took down a book from my store at the window and brought it to Eilis. It was "The Story of Ireland."

"God will reward you," she said. "One gets an indulgence for lending a good book." I was struck by the way she said this and by her eager manner. I took a low stool and sat by her.

She had been reading a story in the summer, and she

3

began to tell me the story eagerly. It was commonplace enough as written, probably a story out of some English newspaper, but Eilis told it as a folk-tale, and it became full of color and wonder. I knew by her gesture and by her care for the good word that she had listened to the poets and had heard the talk of scholars. She had the old culture, I thought, so I spoke to her in the Irish I was learning. But after we had exchanged some phrases, she said, as she took up her work, "Acushla, it's a long time since I spoke the Gaelic. The words are like the words of my old songs; I can hardly bring them to mind."

I knew her for Eilis Nic Ghabhrain—Elish MacGovern, as the people now called her. The MacGovern name had associations for me, for it was connected with that culture which the country people still hold, fragments of some long-descended civilization, Celtic or what you will. Phelim MacGovern, the brother of Eilis, was, to my mind, a good representative of this peasant culture. He lived at the time when the peasants were making an entry into affairs. A nation had been born in the shadow of past defeats and was beginning to stir. As yet the struggle was for a little security, a little knowledge, a little toleration. The tenant-farmers of Ireland were closing up for the bitter struggles against feudal privilege; they had not enough detachment to realise the nation. Phelim MacGovern, a poet and a scholar, understood the national idea, but this understanding brought him into frequent conflict with interests that were growing up in his community. He was often the object of powerful satire, for his neighbours delighted in a vigorous presentation of certain humours, and Phelim was always good material. However, he was a personality to the people, and it was likely that tradition would leave him a personality to their children. His poems are still in the minds of some of the older people of the Midlands. "The Lament for William Conroy, who was transported" is the best of Phelim MacGovern's poems.

He had met his end long before my meeting with Eilis, his sister, who was now an old woman. It was a tragic end, but it does not concern this story. I knew Phelim for a while when he was an old man. He used to repeat Latin poetry for me, and passages from the Irish version of the Iliad. His sister, too, had brought something down from this culture of the old days.

I gave more attention now to Eilis. There was grace and charm about this woman of eighty. Generally the older women in this part of the country have the manner that comes from a fine tradition; they have, too, the repose that comes with age, the acceptance, the trust. Eilis had these, and some other graces as well; a happy laugh, a gesture that seemed out of her girlhood, something wayward. My aunt was minding the bread, and the children were quiet. Eilis had quieted them. She remained watchful of the children, and now and then she would speak to them, or give them some task.

"Indeed, it was our house you were in, the day you stood out of the rain," said Eilis, "and it was my daughter you saw. It is desolate now, my house, for it's too far away from people. My daughter married a man from the town, a dark man. I don't understand him at all, and how could I, for he's not like another. He takes no notice of the land and has no care for it; I don't think he understands it at all. He'd say, 'Here's a paper for the reading woman,' or, 'Make room for the learned woman,' by way of making a mock of me.

"I think I'm like little Margaret here, who does be longing for a house by the roadside, the way she could be watching the people pass. Often, in my own mind, I see the house I was born in. It was white and high, in the friendly county of Fermanagh. There were trees around the house, and inside there was room after room. I had a room for myself in that house. Hadn't I the courage to leave the place where I was a girl, and to come here with a strange man, marrying away, and so far from my own people?

"The people here are good, and over-good, and Michael Conroy, my husband, was the best of them all. A man that wouldn't let me break a sod of turf across my knee, he took such care of me. It's no wonder I got fond of him, though for a long time my girl's heart was back in Fermanagh. Troubles grew up there. It's a long time ago now, and I don't think you ever heard about the happenings there. An election brought the troubles on. A man from the people went up against the landlord, and the gentry tried to frighten the people about voting for him. My father was asked to vote for the landlord, but he wouldn't go with that party at all. They broke him of his lands, and they put him out of his house, and they destroyed his trade with that. For my father had rich lands, and they were the greatest loss maybe, but I can't help thinking of the house that was so white and so fine. There were trees around it, as I told you, and you would have to open seven gates before you came to the door. Twelve of my father's children could sit down at his table. Eighteen persons worked in his house, for my father was a weaver by trade, getting good money for their work and their yarn. My father's father, and seven fathers beyond that, had lived there, and eight women of our name had kept fire on that hearth. And, maybe, the thorn-bushes that the travelling-man told me about are growing out of that hearth now. God have mercy on the people whose hearts and hands were against that house!

"Michael Conroy was good to me, and he was good to my people. When my father was broke of his lands he had his trade still. Michael built him a house behind our own, so that my father could have a place to work in. My father lived there, at the back of us, and he began to get the custom of the neighbours around. But he was broken in his strength and it wasn't months before he got bad in health. In a while it came to the priest's turn, and my father was anointed. I said to my man, 'If my father is to die, I would like him to die under our roof.' Michael stood up, the man who never denied me anything, and he went to the door. Something put it into my mind to go over to him again. 'It will bring a blessing to our children,' I said. He went out.

"In a while Michael was back. He carried my father across the fields. 'Sister,' said he (he always called me sister), 'wipe the sweat off my face.' My father was on his back, and I wiped the sweat off my man's face. We put my father to bed, and he died in the night. The week after that Michael Conroy, my husband, was buried.

"There was no child, and there was no blessing on the house. I ran away from the house for the comfort I could get from my mother. She was living with a son of hers in the County Cavan. Many's the time after that my head was on her lap. I could hear the people say: 'She's too young to be a widow; she'll have to marry again if it was only for the sake of the fields.' Then my uncle went to Michael's place, and he got the fields ready. He couldn't get hands enough to spread the manure. He came back and told my mother that I'd have to marry. I suppose the pain was wearing away. My uncle went to the priest, and between them they got a good man for me. In a year I was married again, and back in Michael's house."

Eilis spoke to the children, and then went on with her knitting in silence. "Well, since that everything I saw was good, except we'd be lonesome at times when someone would die. I wonder are the young so kind? I often think that the world has knocked the friendship out of the people.

"And now I'll tell you why I was so loth to leave the County of Fermanagh. I wasn't fond of Michael Conroy; indeed, I didn't think of him at all when he came to our place in the beginning. Besides, the boy wanted more of a fortune with me than my father was willing to give. The match was broken off three times for the difference of five pounds, and when he went away that time I thought I had seen the last of Michael Conroy. One Sunday morning I was coming from early Mass, and my comrade girls were with me. I saw the cars before our door, and the crowd of strangers, and I knew that the Longford people had come back. My mother was watching out for me. She drew me aside, and she brought me into the barn. 'Conroy agrees, and your father agrees,' she said, 'but Eilis, my heart, I know that it's Shaun Gorman you're fond of. I'll send for him,' she said, 'and in God's name let the two of you go away together. You could go to his people, and the Gormans will be strong enough to mind you.' 'Mother,' said I, 'let me do my father's bidding.' "

"Was your mother wrong?" I asked. It was so far back now I could ask her. "Were you in love with Shaun Gorman?"

"I was, and greatly in love with him," said said.

"Was he fond of you?" I asked.

"How are we to know the heart of a man?" she said. "Shaun Gorman would be up to see the first smoke rising out of our house. He knew every scallop in the thatch, he had watched to see me at the door so often."

"And why wouldn't you take your mother's counsel and go with him?"

"I told it to my mother and we standing there in the barn. 'Mother,' I said, 'I'll tell you everything, and then we'll go to the people who have come for me. Mother, Shaun Gorman and myself planned to run off together. Do you remember when Maurya, the servant girl, went over to Shaun's house, and I went for her in the evening? When I went out of this house I brought all I cared for with me, and I was to go with Shaun Gorman that night. But when I came to the ditch between his fields and our own, my knees failed, and I couldn't pass. I made the sign of the Cross, and I tried again, and again my knees were loosened. Then I said a prayer to the Virgin Mary, and after I said it every limb of me trembled. I sat down, and I could hear the moving of the horse that was to carry us to Shaun's people. The horse was before the door of his house. There was only a ditch between Gorman and myself, but the will of God was against it all. I rose up and came away. Maurya came back by herself, and when she came into the house she said to me, "Shaun Gorman has done with you, Eilis Mac-Govern, for this night you betrayed him." Shaun doesn't believe that now,' I said to my mother. After a while I put myself in his way, and I told him how it was with me. All he said was, 'It's no matter to me now; it's all over now.'

"I didn't think loath of leaving the sweet County of Fermanagh, where every face had something to say of Shaun Gorman. I heard the voices making a bargain. Then I heard Michael Conroy's, and I liked the kindness in that voice. I took my mother's hand, and the two of us went into the house."

The FLUTE PLAYER'S STORY

THERE IS A ROAD in Kerry which seems to have been invented by some racial spirit, so that the Wanderlust might be perpetuated in us. When you set foot on that road you go on till the sense of its endlessness wearies you. You stop, but your spirit is still upon the road. Sometimes you meet people, women generally, driving asses. They are in twos and threes making some journey together. Once I asked one of these women where the road went when it crossed the hills. She had never heard. I asked her what was the nearest town along the road. She gave it a soft monosyllabic name. I asked her how long in her opinion, it would take me to get to that town, walking. She said, in Irish, "My treasure, if you were to set out now (it was in the early afternoon), you would be in the town with the daylight." I never reached the town with the soft monosyllabic name. One day I went far along the road. I had passed where the lake had made a beach for itself. There was a wide bog on both sides of me, and before me were the silent enfolding hills. I saw a figure huddled by the grass of the ditch. Before I came near it a cyclist policeman had swooped down, and the figure was on its feet. A man stood in the middle of the road swaying about, a corpulent figure, big and round of stomach. I perceived that his chin had many folds, that his eyes were small and dead-looking, that in spite of his watch-chain, his manners were obsequious. I could not rid my mind of the impression that this man was somehow connected with the sea. Yet it was impossible to imagine such a creature on board ship. He was of the docks rather than of the ocean. He might be a person who had drowsed and fattened in some little marine store. Evidently the policeman wanted the man to move somewhere; yet there were three very good reasons for the man's inertia. In the first place, he was as gross as matter; in the second place, he was lame of a leg; in the third place, he was drunk. I heard the policeman ask him where he had spent the previous night. The man, bringing, as it were, thought-particles from afar off, informed the law that the town of Ballinasleeve was his last abiding place. Ballinasleeve is in the inhabited country which I had just left behind. "And are you a tradesman?" asked the policeman. With ponderous gravity the man replied, "Well, no, sir, I am not a tradesman. I am a musician, a strolling musician. Sir, I play upon the flute."

A musician! A strolling musician! One that made music on a flute! If incongruity is humour, here was comedy indeed. The policeman spoke out of a great amaze! "A musician—a strolling player! Do you tell me that?"

"Sir," said the man, "why would I be deceiving a policeman? Here is my instrument." He took out of his breast-pocket a flute. The policeman examined it incredulously, while the strolling player, hat in hand, wiped his head with a red pocket-handkerchief. His bald head shone in the evening sun.

"Can you play on this?" the policeman inquired.

"I can," said the musician. "Drunk or sober I can play on the flute. Sometimes I can play better than at other times. I could play better after a sleep." The policeman gave him back his flute. The man turned to go. He turned toward Ballinasleeve and the abodes of men.

"Stop," said the law. "I thought you told me that you had spent the night in Ballinasleeve?"

"Yes, sir; I spent the night in the town of Ballinasleeve."

"Well, then, move the other way," said the policeman. He mounted the machine. The man swayed about. Then he moved some paces in obedience to the edict. I noted that the policeman had risen above local and temporal law. He had expressed the eternal and the universal law. "You must move to live." In obedience to this the artist took a few steps into the wilderness. Then he plunged forward, and lay face downwards in the ditch. I went on, meditating on the law.

Coming back along the road I heard the sound of a flute. The artist was playing to some workers in a far-off bog. His head was bare and shining. The red handkerchief was about his neck. He had worked himself into a mild ecstasy, and was capering about on the road. He sat down by the side of the road. I went and sat near him.

"It's well for you that has the music," I said to him in Irish.

"The music that I play is not the best of music," said the man, speaking in Irish also. "But the people of the country like it."

"You have good Irish," I said, "but I don't think you're a Kerry man."

"I'm a long time on the roads of Kerry," he said. I asked the man for the time. He drew out a large silver watch, and told me the hour. I watched the mountain across the lake. The side of it was brown, steeped in the rays of the sun. The little bunches of sheep seemed to crawl up and down. I loafed, and invited my soul to loaf. I talked to the musician about fiddles, flutes, and that musical instrument which is becoming national and typical in the province of Munster, the melodion. The man's soul was not on fire for his art; he talked about it in the most objective and material way. He was certainly no Munster man. His brain did not fling out words joyously. No word he said hinted the man's dream of himself. There he sat by the side of the road, talking, as if newly taken out of some dark little hand-me-down shop, or some little eating house, that had for a sign the cup and saucer. Still we gossiped for a long time. At last there was movement on the road. A van was going towards Ballinasleeve, one of these wagons that hold the side show of a fair, and is a travelling house beside it. It was a red van with a little flue, drawn by a small and tired horse. A man and woman walked beside the van, and I recognised them for Mr. and Mrs. Antinous, circus people, and friends of mine. The flute player recognised them too, and the recognition brought a dull, malignant look to his face. The couple drew near, Mrs. Antinous was a heavy figure, with a grotesque dress, stiff and black. Her husband was smoking and chirping as usual. How well I remembered Sammy, the Cockney husband of Mrs. Antinous. Sammy, was stone-deaf, but he apprehended certain things by a sort of heightened sensibility. Thus if you said, "What's the drinks?" or "The same again," Sammy drew himself from the remotest corner of the shop, and stood before the counter without a word. I observed the one horse with interest. When I met the couple last in the County of Cavan the horses were five, and had recently been seven. Poor Mrs. Antinous! Her state had shrunk to this little measure. She walked along stolidly, but to me she was a tragic figure.

They greeted me, and I stood talking to them for a while. The flute player remained, big and ugly, in the ditch. Mrs. Antinous recognised him. She stopped her husband's idle chatter, and pointed out the musciian. Sammy took the pipe out of his mouth, and twisted on his feet with a sort of pixie-glee. "It's William Ferguson," he said. "The missus' valentine," he said. "She's the honeysuckle and he's the bee; he, he, he!" Mr. Antinous went over to the ditch. "How are you, William," he said. "It's a long time since we met, William." William remained in the ditch as silent as a frog of the marsh. Mrs. Antinous gripped her protector by the hand, and led him away, but Sammy was irrepressible. He turned his head many times as they went down the road. "William," said he, "the missus and myself desires you to afternoon tea. We'll send the ambulance for you, William." The flute player by this time had gathered his words together, "Go on," said he, "yourselves and your one horse." He turned on me as I came up, the dull, malignant look still on his face. "It's a hired horse, too," he said; "it's a horse of Flannagan's. Let her go. Maybe I'll stroll into the town to-morrow, and see what herself and him will be doing at the fair. They'll have a little stand, and bottles for the men to throw rings over and the like. They'll make little at that. There's little drinking in the town now. The whole country has the mission-pledge. Where there isn't drinking there isn't sport, and it's no good having a shooting range or a little gallery. They're very low in the world. Would you believe it, sir, I once offered myself in marriage to that woman?

"You've probably heard about me from certain parties that you're acquainted with, but one story is good until another is told. My name is William Ferguson. I'm from Scotland. I came from the city of Paisley. I was barbering for a while, but I was sacked from that because the proprietor thought I wasn't sociable enough for a barber. Then I was in the betting line, but the police came against me there. I came to Ireland with a gang of harvesters. I played for them on the flute. Then I settled down to live in Kerry. I got a bed here and there, and the people gave me the bit to eat. They have dances at certain places at this time of the year, and they make up a little collection for the musician. As the woman gone by, I met her after I was a while in Kerry. She was a young widow then, with a husband after dying on her. Her husband was a man you may have heard of. Sarsfield was his name.

"This Sarsfield died, and his widow would be well off if a woman could manage the circus business. She had a tarpaulin that would cover a field. It was worth a lot of money. She had an organ worth close on fifty pounds. It was played by steam. She had fifteen horses. I heard about Mrs. Sarsfield in a house where I was taking a drink, and I thought that a job under her would be worth something. I went round, and asked for a job, and she put me collecting at the tent. She put another man to watch me. I held onto the job. You know, sir, that every man likes to settle down in life, and for that reason I had thoughts of marrying Sarsfield's widow. I stood a likely chance. A woman can't look after a circus. The men that a woman will pay can't be relied on. It's the same in the barbering business. It's the same in all lines of business, except a pawn-shop. Now a circus is the most difficult line that a woman could handle, because she has to watch both men and horses. I used to say to myself, 'You'll have to marry again, my good woman.' I had a good hand with horses, and that's curious when you think I was born and bred in the city of Paisley. However it is, the horses turn their heads to me when I walk down the street. I took charge of that woman's horses. It's likely she'll deny it now, but I tell you, sir, the horses kept in good shape when I had my hand on them. She couldn't help but notice how careful I was of her property. I mentioned marriage to her in a kind of a way, and in a sort of a way she let me know that she wasn't ready for it. But she soon saw the way things would go, and by degrees I prepared her mind for marriage. There was no arrangement between us. There was a sort of agreement. There was no one except myself she could marry, and she'd have to marry soon.

"It's not the way of men to see anyone else get ahead of them in any way. The other men got jealous of me, and they'd never miss a chance of doing an injury to me. They used to leave me to bring the horses to the river myself. It's hard for a lame man to be legging it after horses. I used to have to give pennies to the boys of the town to give me a hand with the horses. They'd get them down to the river, and draw the water, and I'd manage the horses. It was while I was attending the horses one day that Antinous came up, and offered to give me a hand. He was a poor raggy fellow without a boot on his foot. He was sacked out of the swinging boat business. I knew by the way that he touched horses that he was never used to live animals. I couldn't shake him off, for the man was deaf, and consequently gave no heed to my sayings. He brought the horses up to the tent, and was there before me. Mrs. Sarsfield was at the van, and he was standing before her, bowing like a clown, and pattering away. He said she was the prairie flower, and mind you, the woman listened to him, though she could have heard the same thing in the ring any night.

"I suppose she gave Antinous a job?" I said.

"She gave him a job," said my friend the flute player. "I think he begged the job off her. He told her he had no mother. She gave him the job, and he and me used to take the horses to the water every day. He knew nothing about horses. I let on to be sick one day, and I let him take the horses to the river by himself. It was a stony place. The horses' legs would have been broken only for some of the men gave Antinous a hand out of the ill-will they had for myself. When he came back Mrs. Sarsfield brought him in to tea. I didn't do a hand's turn for her that day, nor the day after. She came out to me then. Mind you, I didn't want to lose my job, but I told her she'd have to get rid of Sammy Antinous, or else part with myself. If she could have seen what would happen to her horses she would have given in. But that wasn't to be seen.

"The end of the story happened in the town of Crossgar. There is a shop there owned by a widow woman by the name of Molloy. When I was in the town I did nothing, but I often used to go into Mrs. Molloy's, and have a few glasses to myself without anyone to disturb me. This night I went in. I had the flute in my hand, and I made my way over to the counter. Before I sat down I looked around, and I saw Sammy Antinous and Mrs. Sarsfield sitting on a bench. Sammy asked me to have a drink, but I refused him. I turned round, and I offered Mrs. Sarsfield what was becoming to a lady, a glass of wine. She accepted my offer and Sammy carried over the glass to her. I didn't drink anything myself, but I sat and watched her for a long time. 'Mrs. Sarsfield,' I said to her, 'this young man can't hear us, so we may as well talk now. Look at him and look at me. He has no head, Mrs. Sarsfield. I'm weak on the legs, but my head is sound. If you want to keep your horses sound marry me, and let me look after them.' She didn't drink at all, but she sat there very miserable. 'I don't know how it is,' she said, 'but I'm more used to this young man than I'm used to you.' Sammy was trying to listen all the time. 'I'm as used to horses,' he said, 'as horses are used to oats. I was managing horses when I was only up to William's leg. 'They were wooden horses,' said I. 'He'll soon get used to live horses, Sammy will,' said the woman. She was very foolish. To the present time Sammy Antinous treats all manner of living horses as if they were wooden horses. Sammy got up to go to the counter, and I saw that Mrs. Sarsfield slipped the money into his hand. I knew she'd have him after that, and there was no use in me waiting on. I turned to that woman, and I spoke words that brought the blush to her cheek. 'Ma'am,' said I, 'I'm sorry to see you behave in the way that a respectable woman would not behave. You're marrying that young man, not that he might keep your little business together, not that he might be a protector to you, not that he might look after your horses. You're marrying him out of the passion of women,' I said; 'and, mark my words, you will call the day cursed. Babylon fell,' I said, 'and Rome fell, and the Scarlet Woman of Rome fell, and you'll fall likewise.' I said no more. I let them go out. I drunk small whiskies, and when I wakened they were gone from the town. At the next station my words came true. A horse broke its leg at the watering place. Ever since they lost horses, one here, and two there. She's going into town now with a hired horse, without a tarpaulin, and without an organ. I doubt if she'll make enough to get the van drawn out of the town."

The flute player ended his story as the wandering moon lifted its fantastic shape above the lake. He rose up then and we went down the road together. Afterwards he had occasion to repeat the good toast which I will set down here.—

> Slan argus seaghal agat;
> Bean ar do mhein agat;
> Talamh gon chios agat,
> Agus bas in Eirinn.

> *Health and life to you;*
> *The woman of your choice to you;*
> *Land without rent to you,*
> *And death in Eirinn.*

MARRIAGE

T HE CUNLIFFE HOUSE was illuminated; a candle was lighted
in the kitchen window, a lamp burned in the upper
bedroom, and another candle in the lower bedroom. This illumination was the sign of some excitement in the house. A
marriage was being arranged, and the party on the other side
were to visit Cunliffe's this evening.

Michael Cunliffe had for living children Martin, John and
Julia, Matt and Rose, Francis, and Ellen. Three were at home,
John, Francis, and Ellen; John was the eldest of these and the
farm would come to him, and Francis was a young fellow
working on land until he could make some settlement for himself. Ellen had just passed the age when she was referred to as
"the gearcallach" and spoken to as "Sis" by the people who
came into the house. She had the look which a Connachtman
saw in the women of the Midlands, *Uisgue faoi thalamh*, "Water
under the ground." This young girl with her copper-coloured
hair and shrewd eyes could hold her own in a game of intrigue.

Although lights were in the windows it was still the early
dusk of an autumn day. Francis had brought up the horse. The
cattle were coming up the long bohereen that led from the
road. Michael Cunliffe walked behind his cattle. On his left
hand were some acres of tumbled bog and waste ground
where rushes stood beside pools of water. The ground on his

right hand showed the black soil of the bog. The potatoes were
being dug, and on the ridge were spectral potato-stalks. Back
of the house there was a tillage field, a pasture field and a
meadow with aftergrass. Forty years before Cunliffe had come
into the place from a neighbouring county. It was after the
famine, land was cheap and he got about thirty acres of land,
good and bad, at a low rent. He had built the house himself; he
had dug the clay out of the pit, mixed it and raised his walls
foot by foot. Friends had helped him to lay the long beams that
held the roof. He had woven branches through the beams and
had his roof thatched with the straw of his crop. Michael Cunliffe had been living with kin of his, the Markeys, and when
the house was built he had married a woman who was a far out
member of the family. Michael's wife was no longer living.

The horse was stabled at the end of the byre. After Francis had gone into the house his father remained with the cattle.
Michael would praise a woman by saying that she was kind to
a cow, or a young man by saying he had a good hand on a
horse. His byre was a second household. He had pride in his
horse and his cattle and he had comradeship with them.

He was stroking down the horse when the car with the
visitors turned off the road on to the bohereen.

The Cunliffes had gone far to make an alliance for John.
They were fairly secure and they expected a good dowry with
the woman that would come into the house. A well-off and
respected farmer in the County Leitrim, John Owens, was on
the look-out for a good match for his daughter Mary, and he
and Michael Cunliffe had come together at fair. Subsequently
John had visited at the Owens' house. Negotiations had
reached the stage when the other party might look over the
Cunliffes' ways and means. Mary was making the visit with
her people. When they came to the yard, Michael came out of
the byre and welcomed them to the place.

John Owens had observed the ground between the road
and the house. They went into the byre and then they looked

at the sow that had her second litter. The car outside and the cart were appraised as good vehicles, the stack of turf showed a plentiful supply, and the hay was well saved. The pair went into the field at the back of the house and looked at two well-grown calves that were on the stubble. Then they went into the meadow and stopped before a young horse.

"He'll be worth twenty pounds at the Fair of Cahirmona," said John Owens.

"More," said Michael Cunliffe.

"Not much more."

"Three pounds more."

"Ay, I'd give that for him." There were a few sheep on the meadow.

"They belong to my son, Francis," said Michael Cunliffe. "He'll be settling for himself soon. Now I'll tell you what's coming to the boy. There's forty pounds in the bank for him, and he has the little stock that you see. There was talk of him marrying a young woman that has a farm beyond this. But I hear that he has fallen into fancy with a girl that's back from America. I believe they'd have enough between them to take a little farm and stock it."

"The girls that come back from America are wasted before they settle down here," said John Owens.

"You're right," said Michael. "But I'd like you to know that whatever happens, Francis won't be taking anything off the farm."

"I like your way of doing," said John Owens, "and I like the look of the place. I'd like half of Mary's fortune to be left with the young people."

"No, John. I won't listen to that at all."

"I want the young people to have the handling of some money."

"Well, there's no use saying one thing and meaning another. I must have the grasp of everything in the place. It all came from me and it all must stay with me as long as I'm above ground. Ellen has to get her fortune out of it, and everything else that's in my purse and place, will go to your daughter and my son."

"How much do you think I'm thinking of giving with Mary."

"Two hundred pounds."

"I'm not altogether as well off as that."

"I won't be bargaining with you. If you don't say two hundred pounds, John, we won't talk of a marriage."

"Well, I'll say two hundred pounds. It's more than we thought of when we were young, but times are changed, and changed for the better, thank God. Two hundred pounds. Here's my hand to you."

"*Saoighail fada agat.*"

Then they went into the house. John and Francis were standing before the fire in the kitchen, and Michael Cunliffe briefly told them the terms of the engagement. He was satisfied. Ellen came from the upper room and announced that supper was ready. Before each place there was a plate of roast goose and ham, and a glass of whisky was beside each plate. Mary was seated with her hands on her lap. She looked at the picture of the Virgin that was over the bed. Under it was a withered branch of last Palm Sunday. Some affection for her surroundings began to come into Mary's mind. John came to her and pressed her to drink a glass of whisky. Her voice was high-pitched with nervousness. "As true as God is over me," she said, "I'll take none." "I'd rather have a girl that drank before my face than the one that would go behind the door and do it," said Michael Cunliffe. "Drink it," said her father. "Stand up with John Cunliffe and drink the glass." "Drink it, Mary, lamb," said her mother. Her face was red with blushes when she drank the glass. Then she sat still and John held her hand. "Long life to ye both," said Michael. "You are both of honest people. And may they be honest, them you leave behind you." Some simplicity in Mary's thought and speech gave Ellen, who had been a monitress in the school, a touch of patronage towards her. She thought of Mary as coming from a remote and uncivilised place, and her want of self-possession seemed part of her barbarism. When the Owens were returning, John Cunliffe went some miles with them. It was near morning when he came back, and he and his father sat talking until they went out to their work.

Two weeks after, John married, and Mary Owens came into Michael Cunliffe's house. Francis got married in the spring. When the elder brother brings in a wife, the young girl who was the daughter becomes the step-daughter of the house. Cunliffe's house no longer stood for a single interest— there was Owen and Mary's interest, there was her father's, and there was Ellen's own interest. The younger girl was subject to Mary. She would be sent out for turf when she wanted to read, and bid milk the cows when she wanted to dress for the evening. These things Ellen had done before, but she had done them in the interest of the indivisible Cunliffe household. Now her duties were a tribute of labour.

She brought in the turf of an evening and sat down by the fire. Bridget Rush was there, and there was no one else in the house. Bridget used to go from house to house, knitting stockings and mending clothes. She was every one's familiar. "I'm thinking of getting a good husband for you, Miss Cunliffe," she said. "Who would he be?" asked Ellen. "A fine young man that has just come back from America." "Hugh Daly, is it?" "Indeed it is Hugh Daly." Ellen had considered Hugh Daly. His American clothes set him off well, and besides, he was a well-built, good-looking fellow. Hugh Daly was settling down on a farm that his father had not minded over-well. But before taking root he had let himself out in two or three drinking bouts, and when in these he had not been behind in using the strong hand. "He'll be a steady man when he begins to put his little place in trim," said Bridget Rush. "They say it's a poor place," said Ellen. "Well, if a woman came in with a fair fortune they could make it a tidy place in a few years." "Katie, his sister, has to get her fortune out of the place," said Ellen. "I'm not asking what your fortune is, daughter," said Bridget Rush, "but your father, sure, would give a fortune with you that would let Hugh settle with Katie, and give ye a good start."

She met Hugh Daly in a house where there was a dance. He addressed her as "Miss Cunliffe," and asked her to dance with him. There was good-humoured swinging and squeezing, but Ellen Cunliffe had a prestige that kept her clear of these familiarities. The girls and the young men went home in groups and not in couples. Hugh Daly walked beside Ellen and two or three other girls. In a week Ellen and her sister Rose knew that he was on for making a match. Sometimes when Ellen was there he would come into Rose's house, and when she was going home he would take the road with her. On a market day in Cahirmona he entertained them, and on the way back he told Rose of his regard for Ellen. It was agreed that he should make a proposal to Michael Cunliffe that week.

He did not tell Rose what dowry he expected with Ellen. These were his circumstances. Hugh Daly's sister lived on the farm, and she would have to get her portion out of it. Moreover, his father had been a drinking man, and the farm was badly wasted. The evening that he went to her father's Ellen stayed at her sister's house. Hugh Daly came in. He was angry; the dowry that her father had spoken of was little. "Your father wants to make little of me," he said. "Eighty pounds is what he'd give for your fortune; no more than that. If it was anybody else that asked for you he'd have said a hundred. The world knows that Katie has to get her money and that there's hardly any stock on the farm." He parted from Ellen, still in a temper.

Ellen cried when he had gone, and for consolation Rose gave her some practical advice. She went back to the house. Her father had to go to a fair early at some far-off place, and he was asleep in the settle in the kitchen. John and Mary were in the room above. She put out the light and sat by the fire that was covered over with ashes. She heard Mary talking in the room above. "Where would she get a hundred pounds when everybody gets their rightful share? My father's money wasn't given to make a big fortune for Ellen Cunliffe." Mary was jealous of the thought that Ellen claimed a dowry that was anything like the dowry she had brought into the house. "Me that had the biggest fortune that came into this townland. Never will Hugh Daly bring her into his house," Mary said again.

She swore by the beam of her father's roof that she would leave that house triumphantly, and marry Hugh Daly. She sat there by the fire until it was nearly dawn. Then her father arose and she got him breakfast. He ate by candlelight. "Hugh Daly," he said, speaking about the young man's visit, "isn't the first that spoke about you." "I wouldn't care to marry any other man," said Ellen. "That's the talk of a young girl." "I'm in earnest, father," she said. When he was going out of the door she put her hands on his face. "I am a young girl," she said, "the youngest you have. And you wouldn't have me stay long in this house and be made little of by the stranger-woman in the room above." Her father made no answer to her. But she saw that he looked back to where she stood in the doorway.

He got a good price for the horse he brought to the fair. That evening, very privately, he gave his daughter ten pounds of the price he had got, and then stood looking out of the window, thinking of the stock which that ten pounds would have helped to buy. "Mary is good," he said to Ellen at another time, "and she means good to you." Ellen's grievance against her sister-in-law was subsiding; she knew that she was good-natured and that she would have to count on her good nature.

She claimed the eggs laid on the farm for her perquisite for the year. Mary did not put any obstacle in the way of her getting them; indeed, she got to be very sympathetic, and would take the eggs to the market herself, as she was better at getting a good price for them than Ellen was. The money got in this way was added to Ellen's dowry. Money was made up, and after a few months Ellen had a dowry that the Dalys would consider. She married Hugh within the year, bringing into the house a dowry of just a hundred pounds.

Ellen is now the mother of five children, and four of them are fine boys. She lives too near her brother's for perfect accord to be between the two families. She does not forget that she came into Hugh Daly's house with a fortune less than he asked, or that the portion she brought was made up with a contribution from the share going to Mary and John. She has the mocking tongue that often breaks the peace between the two houses. At school her children are kept in competition with Mary's children, who are rude and somewhat dull. Michael, Mary's eldest boy, was in Ellen's house one evening when I was there. He had given a foolish answer to the priest, who had spoken to the children on the road. Ellen was laughing over the adventure, but she had a laugh that left it hard to say whether she laughed with the boy or laughed at him. Michael knew enough of his aunt to discover the mockery in her mind. "Do you ever say your prayers, Ellen!" said he. "I do, in troth," said Ellen. "I'll tell you, Michael," said she, "what I prayed for last night. I prayed that I would see ten cows, a horse and car before this house, and that I would see your place with only an ass and a goat. But Michael, a chara," said she, "I'm only talking. We're the one blood, and what could I wish but good luck to you?" She was sincere in both attitudes. And before Michael went she was teasing him again. Her formula reminded me of the opening of that splendid tale, "The Little Brawl of Allen." "Well, thanks be to God," said Finn, "we're all at peace. It's a long time since we were at peace before. Indeed, we weren't at peace, Goll, since the day I killed your father."

MARCUS of CLOONEY

H E BEGAN IN THIS WAY. He said, "Martin Fallon, my uncle, is the brother of Hugh Fallon, the grazier. You probably know Martin Fallon: a strong farmer and a man of cows. I have known my uncle for twenty-five years. In the course of a quarter of a century I have seen only one variation in my uncle's appearance. To all appearance his clothes are always the same clothes, and his beard is always in the same stage of growth. You have seen him at the fair, and you will have noticed that he always carries the same ash-plant, that his coat is always of the same blue-black material, and that his waist-coat is of corduroy, that it is sleeved, and that his trousers are of corduroy also. One morning lately I awakened in my uncle's house in Aughnalee. As my faculties were slowly flowing back to me the door opened, and my uncle entered the room softly. He was translated. He carried a stick; and the stick was even changed: it was not the familiar ash-plant, it was a black-thorn, and it had a silver band near the top. His coat was of a deeper tint of blue, and of a more grandiloquent cut. His waist-coat was black; it was cut low, and showed a wide expanse of starch shirt. Below the shirt there was room for a massive chain of silver. His trousers hung with a remarkable perpendicularity; and such was the condition of his boots that I marvelled that I had not been awakened by the rubbing and the accompanying reverberations. He was shaved, not here and there as was his immemorial custom, but with a clear and exhaustive sweep. He had on a hat, black, high-crowned, and of a remarkable width of brim. He went to the mirror and surveyed himself from various points of view. He took off his hat and said, 'In the name of God.' Then he went out of the room, closing the door softly behind him.

"Now my uncle could not be making preparations for marriage, for that excellent woman, my aunt, is still in being. He was not going to arrange a marriage for either of his sons— they have not come to a marriageable age—nor was he going to take a daughter to a convent. Why then this laborious transformation? and why was my uncle going abroad on the first clear day, and the potatoes awaiting spraying?

"The mystery drew me from bed. As I was eating my breakfast my aunt conveyed clues by many hints. My uncle was an ambassador. On account of his silence and discretion he had been selected to go on a mission. The mission was to the house of our parish priest. The mission was undertaken on behalf of a certain young man, newly returned from America. The negotiation on which my uncle had entered would be long, it would have many stages, its ultimate object, however, was a meeting between the priest's niece and the young farmer, whose name was Stephen Geoghan. Then there would be a conference between the elders with a view to arranging a marriage.

"When I understood the situation," said Farral Gilroy, "I went outside, sat on a ditch, and pictured to myself the opening negotiations. My uncle enters to Father Gilmartin. It would be after breakfast, and the priest would be reading a Latin tome. Father Gilmartin is a student of Aquinas. He has encouraged the co-operative movement, since he discovered in the Summa the metaphysic of co-operation. But you are not to picture the priest as a worn student; Father Gilmartin is old and heavy; his body moves slowly; and his mind, clear and definite as it is, moves slowly also. Imagine the contact of the two minds in this novel and complex subject. In the terms of the case the negotiations would be delicate, the terms elusive. And Father Gilmartin was appallingly deaf. The meeting, as I saw it, was fundamental as opposed to accidental comedy.

"My uncle returned. The negotiations had been long and uncertain. Miss Casey, Father Gilmartin's niece, was going back to Dublin on Wednesday next; but a meeting between herself and Mr. Geoghan had been arranged. The lady, her brother, Father Casey, and Father Gilmartin would pass through the town of Clooney on their way to the railway station. They intended to call at the house of Marcus O'Driscoll. Mr. O'Driscoll was a close friend of the Geoghan's. Stephen could call in on Wednesday, and thus the parties would meet informally at the house of a mutual friend. The plan commended itself to my aunt. So much was accomplished, and my uncle's reputation would not be submitted to a further strain. The affair was now with God and Marcus O'Driscoll. Mr. Stephen Geoghan then came in. After salutations my uncle silently produced the whiskey. He alluded to the respectability of Miss Casey's family, to the numerous priests that that family had produced, to the fact that Miss Casey was related, not remotely, to a bishop. He alluded in guarded terms to her probable dowry. He dwelt on her good looks, her education and refinement. Thus he worked up to the triumph of his own diplomacy. My uncle left down the glass and grasped Stephen by the hand. 'Be at Marcus O'Driscoll's on Wednesday,' he said, 'and there you'll meet the young lady, with her uncle, the priest, and her brother, who is a priest, too.' I went out then and left them to their conference. I saw my uncle standing at his door watching Stephen Geoghan starting for the house of his friend, Marcus O'Driscoll. My uncle had not yet taken off his official garb. There was a glow of satisfaction about the whole of the man. In such a warm glow I wish to leave my uncle. You will observe that our family comes out of the affair with credit and with an enhanced reputation.

"I now take up with that remarkable friend, Marcus O'Driscoll. Fortunately for my story you know him. Otherwise

it would be difficult for me to shadow forth the personality of
Marcus O'Driscoll, Marcus of Clooney. I would have to discover a language at once exuberant and discreet. You remember the last time we fell in with Marcus; he had been unfolding
to a companion a scheme of agrarian reform based on state
purchase, and he went back on the argument for our benefit.
He spoke weightily, insinuatingly with intimacy. When he
heard your name he had excellent advice to offer as to your
attitude towards Trinity College. It was Marcus of Clooney
who advised Mr. Parnell on a celebrated occasion. I can see him
now in the street of Clooney, speaking to the chief, respectfully, deferentially. His attitude would be that of the private
soldier to whom an accident has given the key to the enemy's
position. His advice would be respectful and disinterested. You
would guess that Marcus O'Driscoll is from the south. As a
matter of fact he is from Munster. He has been close up forty
years among us; but he still regards himself as a stranger in our
midst. He has confided to me that, with the best will in the
world, he cannot quite understand our Leinster type. He finds
us very clannish; and our conduct, political and private, has
often been a disappointment to him. In spite of our clannish-
ness, Marcus O'Driscoll had created for himself an extensive
acquaintance amongst our people. He was very intimate with
the elder Mr. Geoghan, and always professed a great regard for
the son. He received Stephen warmly. That young man beat
about the bush for nine-tenths of his visit, but at least he informed Marcus of the lie of matters. Marcus received the information with becoming discretion. He said little. He walked
down the street with Stephen, and shook hands with him
many times. He then went back to his shop, and with unex-
hausted vitality listened to an old woman's story of how her
chickens had perished of an unknown disease. He called in a
friend who was passing by, and advised him not to let the
doctors interfere in a family case. Afterwards he arranged a
course of conduct for a grazier who was anxious to surrender a
farm. Could the destiny of the house of Geoghan be in safer

hands? Marcus was a vital personality. He was, at it were, discretion become self-conscious.

"The representative of the house of Geoghan is unknown to you. Stephen has a good position. He is a good-looking young man, but one who is hesitant and extremely self-conscious. Stephen's self-consciousness has been increased since his return from America. He brought back a stock of American clothes; and he dresses in the American fashion. He has always the consciousness that the town is agape at his appearance. Really the sensation has long been exhausted; and the town only thinks of him as a young man who calls for 'cocktails' when he wants 'half-ones.' On Wednesday morning he took a new suit out of his trunk and dressed himself carefully. He had intended to drive into Clooney; but, by the time the horse and car had been got ready, he had come to the conclusion that a vehicle in the street would be an embarrassment. He took his bicycle out; but reflection told him that a bicycle would leave him in town too early. He decided to walk. He turned back from the gate to put on a pair of leggings. The leggings were yellow, like the washed leg of a duck. Stephen Geoghan was tall and of a good figure; the leggings and the American suit became him very well. He was such that any girl might take a fancy to him. He walked into the town.

"Stephen walked to the town, his thoughts scattered like sheep on the hill. He paused when he came in sight of Clooney: he was overcome by the sight of that wide, open street. Then he made up his mind to advance boldly, and go into the house of Marcus O'Driscoll. He would probably have done this if he had not become conscious of his leggings at this moment. They were bound to attract attention. The people would stand in the doors, or in groups in the street, and watch him pass. They would see him go into Marcus O'Driscoll's shop. If Miss Casey had arrived the mind of the town would jump to his errand. 'Marcus O'Driscoll is making a match for the Yank.' 'Will the christening be with cocktails, I wonder?' No, he couldn't face the town. He turned to the hedge and plucked out a branch of woodbine, and considered his next move. He elaborated a course of conduct: he would walk into the town as if he had come for the sport of the thing; he would go into a newspaper shop near and go over the sporting papers; then, at the time when Father Gilmartin and Miss Casey would be making a start, he would stroll over as far as Marcus's shop; Father Gilmartin would then introduce him to Miss Casey; Stephen would also be going to the railway station, and would get a lift in Father Gilmartin's car; he would go as far as Maryboro with the party—thus Miss Casey and he would make acquaintance, informally and agreeably, and he would have ample time to talk over affairs with Miss Casey's male relations. It is agreeable to approach these things in curves. The man is foolish who attempts to reach ends by straight lines, for the earth is a curve. Besides, with this plan he could arrange things better himself without the help of Marcus O'Driscoll. 'Better do without that fellow,' thought young Geoghan; 'he'd never let me forget that I was under a compliment to him. He'd tell the town that it was he got the last hundred thrown in. By God, he'd want the first child christened Marcus. It will be a great surprise to O'Driscoll that I'm able to do things out of my own brain. But I wasn't across the Atlantic Ocean for nothing.' Young Geoghan spoke out of the fundamental ingratitude of humanity. In this mood of his we may note that spiritual defect which is, perhaps, the root of tragedy.

"He went into the newspaper shop near, and took up a sporting paper. He stood reading the paper, his legs wide apart, and the lower ornaments were very conspicuous to those in the street, if there were any who cared to note them. He read one paper, left it down on the counter; then he took up another sporting paper; then he said to the girl:—

" 'Do the priests here mind you stocking these papers?'

" 'Not a bit,' the girl returned.

" 'Do you think Father Gilmartin would mind this paper?' Stephen pursued.

" 'I couldn't tell you,' said the girl frankly.

" 'Did you hear that Father Gilmartin was to be in the town to-day?'

" 'Well, no, I didn't. He didn't come yet, anyway,' said the girl.

" 'I suppose you see everyone who comes in?'

" 'Well, indeed I do.'

"Stephen sat and waited. After a while he began to doubt the girl's information as to Father Gilmartin. He began to feel certain that the party had arrived, and were now at Marcus O'Driscoll's. But everyone who came into the shop were unanimous in the opinion that Father Gilmartin wasn't in the town. The sands were running out. Stephen would soon have to call at O'Driscoll's if he were to meet the party at all. He strolled out of the shop. He reflected that it would not look well to make O'Driscoll's a secondary place of call. The best thing to do was to go a little way back, re-enter the town, and go straight to Marcus O'Driscoll's. Stephen turned his back to Marcus O'Driscoll's. As he came to the country road he saw coming towards him the man himself. Marcus shook hands with Stephen. He gave him a pressure long and silent. The handshake said: 'My poor fellow!' Audibly Marcus said.—

" 'Always bring a stick with you when you are walking. And a stick is especially needed along these roads. You're always going up a hill. A stick helps you along more than you'd be inclined to think. Besides, a stick is a comfort when you're by yourself, or on a dark night. It's company; it's like having a dog with you. In my own part of the country no one would go anywhere without a stick; but you can get a good class of a stick in the south of Ireland. I never saw an American stick that I would care to carry. Maybe you have no other sticks except American sticks.'

"Stephen said that he had brought a cane stick back with him.

" 'They're no good,' said Marcus. 'John's James brought one of them back to me, but I never used it. I'll send it over to you some day. It has a silver mount that is nice enough. But the stick you'd cut yourself is the sweetest stick you could carry. Sit down, now, and I'll give you the signs and tokens of a good stick.'

"They sat down on the ditch, Stephen yielding himself with a prayer that Marcus would soon reach the limit of his disinterestedness. They would soon have to be going to Marcus's house. If there were people for the Dublin train a start would soon have to be made.

" 'I believe,' said Marcus, 'that every man ought to cut his own stick. It will come to his hand better afterwards. Now, if you are going to cut a stick about this place, there are only three kinds of timber that you need take into account, and I'll tell you about them now. The hazel makes a satisfactory stick; it's light, and you can cut one with a middling good knife. I heard of a man who cut an ash-plant—cut it, mind you. Always pull an ash-plant. Take one about four feet high and pull it up from the roots. If the root doesn't suit you, pull another. Ash-plants are as plenty here as the stones on the road. I brought a fine blackthorn with me from the south but it's the hardest thing in the world to keep a good stick. Blackthorns grow straight up in some places. Pick one out that's well furnished with thorns. Thorns are the sign of a good stick. Take a little saw with you to cut it. I doubt if you would have a knife that would cut a blackthorn.'

" 'I'll remember that,' said Stephen, and he rose.

" 'Wait a while,' said Marcus. 'Be careful to cut the stick to your own height. A stick from three feet nine to four feet or four feet and half an inch would just suit you.'

" 'Let us go back to the shop,' said Stephen.

"Marcus rose. 'Another thing about sticks,' he continued, 'when you get your stick bend it to a handle. Put a crook on it. A crook gives you a nice handling on a stick.'

"It was at this moment that a car dashed up. There was a priest and a young lady in the car. For a moment Stephen's heart stood still. But the priest was not Father Gilmartin. The car passed, Marcus O'Driscoll making a salute, grave and sub-dued. "Pon my word,' said Stephen, 'I thought I was going to see Father Gilmartin.

" 'He'd have come in only for the Parish Conference,' said Marcus. 'Isn't it queer to think that you might be living ten years next to Martin Fallon, and he'd never give you any ad-vice about a stick.'

" 'Stop,' said Stephen, 'who are them gone by in the car?'

" 'Father Casey and Miss Casey, to be sure,' said Marcus.

" 'And why didn't you bring me to the shop?'

" 'And didn't I see you coming from the shop, man?'

" 'I wasn't in the shop at all,' said Stephen.

" 'Is that the sort of fellow you are?' said Marcus O'Dris-coll. 'There you were, mooning about, and anyone would have thought that something had come between you and the girl.'

" 'And you kept me here blathering about sticks.'

" 'Blathering about sticks! Didn't I talk to you the way I'd talk to any young man that I'd see walking out by himself without a stick?'

" 'It's the like of you that has this country the way it is,' said Stephen, and he turned on his heel. Marcus O'Driscoll stood for a moment looking after him. Then he walked down the street slowly. He stood before his shop door.

" 'He's like the rest,' he said; 'they're all the same: all trick-o'-the-loops and three-card men. They're deserving of nothing but the government they have, and may they long have such to rule over them.'

"Marcus was magnanimous still. There was nothing per-sonal in his resentment."

LAND HUNGER

ONE RARELY SAW MICHAEL HEFFERMAN apart from his son Hugh. Hugh was less of a personality than his father, but in a crowd of Connacht people he was noticeable for his quiet manner; he always seemed a little withdrawn from the life of the fair or the spree. You might describe Hugh Heffernan as a "soft young fellow." He did not look robust, and there was something of solicitude in the way that his father watched him. Michael Heffernan was typical of his people. He had the peasant face, broad and shrewd, the deepset, humorous eyes, and the resolute mouth. He had been away from the land for years. . . . After the death of his wife, Michael went to England, and he had worked in a dockyard amongst aliens. He had come back to Connacht to mind the child, he said. The child had called him, surely, but the land had called him, too. The little house on the wet hillside, the patch of land around, had drawn Michael Heffernan as the ship draws the sailor, as the barrack draws the soldier. Michael had nature for the land, as they say. I do not know what visionary faculty he possessed, but I venture to think that beyond the smoke of the shipping town, Michael Heffernan often saw the potatoes become green on the ridge and the oats turn from green to yellow. This man had no affinity with his companions nor his English surroundings, and the money paid to him was only little coins. He wanted to see his labor grow into something; become crop and harvest. And so he came back to the deep soil, to the smell of the earth, to the satisfaction of being over the sod. He came back to his farm, and his child. Tenderly he reared one, shrewdly he worked the other. Hugh had grown up; he was now a young man of twenty-three, and father and son were inseparable. They lived together and alone. A neighbour woman milked the cow and made the cake for them.

The Heffernans had only four acres of land; they were pinched between a mountain and a grazing farm. On the day of his return Michael Heffernan walked through his own little holding and saw the rich land beyond, vacant except for cattle. From that day he hungered for more land. To have ample land, and with the land to have cattle and horses. No man had a better eye for a beast, no man had a better hand on a horse. He would walk up and down the fair watching the cattle and the horses and going over their points. His own holding could only support a cow, a calf, an ass, and some sheep. We realise the pinch of small holdings when we consider what the lack of a horse meant to the Heffernans. It meant that the tillage of the farm must be done with the spade, and this is an enormous tax in labor. Many's the time Michael Heffernan let his spade lie while he watched the horses of the rich farmer plough up the ridge of the hillside. Isn't it well for them who can yoke horses to their plough! The horses go before you, turning up the earth; so much done, so little labor on yourself. The wide space of ground, the horses, the plough, had an imaginative value for Michael Heffernan. To this child of the earth to plough with horses was poetry and ritual.

Michael had often to compare Hugh's living with the living enjoyed by the young men working in the dockyards of England. He would see Hugh going out in the morning without a rasher to his breakfast and without an egg three days in the week. Hugh was ill one time and Michael had to ask milk from a neighbour. Coming back, he looked across the grass lands adjoining his holding. He saw the calves sucking milk from the cows. Michael Heffernan was filled with the indigna-

tion of the Prophets in the Old Testament. It was as if you had
seen a riotous youth trampling a loaf in the gutter. Christians
without the milk of a cow!

The sight entered Michael Heffernan's heart. It went towards making him the prophet of an agrarian agitation. Soon
after this there was a meeting in the Chapel yard—a lecturer
had come to tell the people of a new method of spraying
potatoes. Some of the speakers referred to the possibility of a
certain Land Department taking over Lord Clanwilliam's estate
and redistributing the land amongst those whose holdings
were not up to the economic standard of twenty acres. Michael
Heffernan was moved to speak. He spoke with the power of a
man who feels deeply. Let them divide the land and give poor
people a chance to live. They were worn out working on their
little farms. They were without proper food; in bad seasons
they were without the turf for the fire. Let them make the
division of the land, and they would have the prayers of the
poor people—ay, and the blessing of God, too, who never
intended that people should have such a poor way of living.
Michael Heffernan's speech found a vigorous response. As a
consequence of the feeling aroused, pressure was brought on
the Land Department to open negotiations with Lord Clanwilliam. One Sunday the priest announced from the altar that
negotiations were proceeding. Michael Heffernan was pro-
foundly moved. When he knelt down again he said a prayer
for success and for God's guidance.

The negotiations bore no fruit for the tenants. A grazier
from the town offered a good rent for the grass and the land
that adjoined Michael Heffernan's holding. It was let on the
eleven months' system. Michael was in town when the news
became known. He hurried back. Standing on a ditch, he saw
the stock put on the farm. There were only fifty head of cattle
brought that evening, and a few sheep and lambs. He went to
the house, and Hugh and himself sat over the fire for a long
time that night. They rested themselves for a while on the bed,
and at daylight they went out. They rounded up the sheep and

the cattle. Early in the morning they were driving the flocks and herds along the road back to the town, five miles away. Men turned back from their journey and joined them. Early workers in the field threw down the spade and went with them. Young men came out of the houses and joined the troop. It was a good-humored, if excited, crowd. Hugh Heffernan was wild with excitement. He shouted and sang songs. Michael went on the march steadily and seriously. He drove Ireton's cattle as though he had been paid for it. He had been reared amongst these friendly beasts, and he could no more injure a cow than he could pass by on the road and see a cow trampling a field of oats. He picked up a lamb and carried it in his arms. With the great, lumbering beasts before them the people came into the town. They brought the cattle up to the grazier's house, and they soon had Mr. Ireton amongst them. In a few words Michael Heffernan told the grazier that the people would not allow cattle on that part of Lord Clanwilliam's estate. The estate must be broken up and divided amongst the people who wanted land.

Next day the original stock and additions were put back on the grass farm. The grazier had invested his money, and was not going to be at any loss. Besides a political party urged him to make a fight and promised him a backing. John Ireton was a man of planter breed. By tradition and connection he belonged to the landlord régime. His connections were amongst bailiffs and agents, and the position and incomes of this class were endangered by land transfer. John Ireton was kindly to his neighbours, but he sincerely distrusted the Celtic peasantry. Between him and them there was a racial antipathy not to be overcome. It was class against class—ay, appetite against appetite. John Ireton stood up for his own appetite and his own class.

It was to the interest of the people to make grazing profitless; therefore though extra police were brought into the district, the cattle were driven again. This time the cattle would not be brought to the grazier's yard; they would be scattered to the four corners of the county. Michael Heffernan told his son to remain at home. Serious and determined himself, he joined the assembly. He drove off a certain number of cattle towards the hills. That day the people came into conflict with the police, and Michael Heffernan was arrested on a charge of inflicting injury on Mr. Ireton's cattle. He was asked to find bail. Michael Heffernan felt very seriously about the cause. He knew the land was not to be won lightly nor without sacrifice. He refused to find bail and he went to jail for a month. Meantime the agrarian trouble came to a settlement. Mr. Ireton surrendered the farm to Lord Clanwilliam, and the landlord reopened negotiations with the Land Department. Michael Heffernan came out of prison, crowds cheering, victory assured. He walked about unsteadily. Hugh came to him, and they left the town and the crowds. There was a darkness of Michael's spirit, the shadow of disgrace and humiliation. He let Hugh talk, saying a few vague words himself now and again. The familiar roads and the growing things brought some restoration.

"Hugh, a chara," said Michael out of a silence, "you will have a good place for yourself some day."

"The sergeant told me that ten acres would be added to our holding," Hugh said.

"Now, isn't that better than an American legacy?" said Michael. He knew that it was better than ten American legacies; an American legacy never brought luck to anyone. But Michael had not begun to think as yet. He could only find formal expressions. "We can keep a horse now," he went on.

"If we had a horse I could earn good money many's a day in the week, drawing goods from the town."

"We will have a beast or a couple of beasts," Michael replied. Father and son walked on in silence. Then Michael said, after a space:

"I saw you with a young woman one Sunday evening, and she was a stranger to me."

"She's by the name of Coyne," Hugh said briefly and formally.

"Maybe she'd be a daughter to Bartley Coyne?" Michael went on.

"She is. She is Bedelia Coyne, and she's back from America a while now," Hugh replied.

"Ay, Bridget Coyne," said Michael, giving her her pre-American name. "She was a good while in America, and all her people had the name of saving."

"She has earned her fortune like many's a girl," said Hugh. There was silence between the two men for a while. Then Michael said:

"I don't care for Yankees, no matter for their fortunes. They're no good about a farmer's house."

"Bedelia Coyne is a good girl," Hugh said, rather warmly. "She's a great favorite with me. And she has a wish for me, too. I know that."

"Please yourself, my son," said Michael. "I'm only thinking about your prosperity. My life wouldn't be any good to me unless I saw you prosperous from this out. Stay on the land awhile and do nothing till we settle down."

That evening Michael Heffernan made a journey over to Coyne's and received something of a state welcome from Bartley and his women folk. He saw Bedelia, and approved of her, although he would have preferred a country girl for his son. Bedelia had distinction in dress and appearance. She was fair, and, like Irish girls of that type who have been for some years in America, her hair and eyes were rather faded. Bedelia was in no hurry back to the States. She had got fond of Hugh Heffernan, the quiet, mannerly, young fellow, and she had made up her mind to marry him.

The young men in the district had attained a certain prosperity. There was talk of marriages and of the building of new houses. Hugh Heffernan and Bedelia Coyne were one of the four couples that got married that summer.

The LITTLE PENSION

A T THE BREAK OF DAY John Greggins turned out of his bed
and went into the apartment that was kitchen and living room. The ballad-singer to whom John had given the
night's shelter was also out of his sleep. Sitting on the sack of
leaves that had been his bed, he was raking away the ashes
that covered the seed of the fire. "Put down a few turf," said
John, "and we'll have an early breakfast." The singer put turf
round the kindlings, while John poured water into the kettle
and hung it above the sods.

"What sort of a night did you put in by this hearthstone?"
asked John.

"A good night," answered the ballad-singer. Then he said
thoughtfully, "you've a lone cricket here that I'd like to marry
to a cricket that's in a house in the County Clare." The singer
was a low-sized fellow, round of limb, and round of body. He
was bare-footed, and wisps of hair fell across his eyes, that
were restless, cunning, and humorous. Maurya, John's sister,
heard the stir, and came down as the kettle was on the boil. A
breakfast of bread and butter, tea and eggs, was made ready
for the man of the house and the guest of the night. The ballad-
singer ate without speaking; outside his songs he had but occa-
sional words in Irish or English. When the meal was finished
he put a ragged cap across his wisps of hair, and went to the
door. "I must be shortening my road now, ma'am," said he,

touching his cap to Maurya, "and I'm thankful to you for what you've bestowed on me." "Easy now," said John; "sure I'll be some of the way with you." He put on his hat, took his stick in hand, and went out with the ballad-singer. That was John Greggins's way; when the beggar, the ballad-singer, or the wandering musician, left his house, John Greggins would rise up and accompany them for miles on the road.

He lived in a place where the very crows were lonely. Perhaps you have no idea of the land where the stones have taken the places of the trees and hedges, where the shadow of a bare mountain is always on an empty lake, where the black of the bog runs into the fields, and where the whole uneven country is under the muffled Connemara sky. John Greggins had no root in the place. The fertile years of his life were passed in the British Army, and it was only since his retirement that he took up this abode with his sister. By a miracle of administration, the State maintained its relations with John Greggins, and once in three months the post came to the house with an installment of his pension.

He came down the mountain path with a good stride; his fine impetuous head held high. The ballad-singer, his eyes fixed on the stretch of the road, kept beside him with a gait that recalled the trot of a dog. "Lift up the music," said John. The singer raised his head and began "The County Mayo." The song was in Irish and this is by way of being its equivalent:—

> Now coming on Spring the days will be growing,
>   And after Saint Bride's Day my sail I will throw;
> Since the thought has come to me I fain would be going
>   Till I stand in the middle of County Mayo!
> The first of my days will be spent in Claremorris,
>   And in Balla down from it I'll have drinking and sport,
> To Kiltimagh then I shall go on a visit,
>   And there, I can tell you, a month will be short.

John Greggins was waving his stick to the music when

the pair came to the road. The singer went on with Raftery's song:—

> I solemnly swear that the heart in me rises
>   As the wind rises up or the mists break below,
> When I think upon Carra and Gallen down from it.
>   The Bush of the Mile and the Plains of Mayo.

"Have you any more of that song?" asked John.

"I have," said the singer.

"Wasn't I lucky to come across you?" said John. "I never heard, at home or abroad, any more than you're after singing."

"There's a verse that has the name of every tree in Ireland, and there's another verse that has the name of every beast in Ireland."

"Raise it, raise it," said John. The singer began:—

> Killeadan's my village and every growth's in it.

Then the song ended. A hare had precipitated itself across the road ahead. The ballad-singer stopped on the road. "I'm going no farther along the road," he said. "I'm going to see a smith this side of the country." With that he crossed the ditch and went on a roving way. The little fellow had scruples about crossing the track of a hare.

John Greggins stood in the middle of the road. The sunlight was no longer lost in the lake, and it was visibly steeping itself in the bog. In the spacious light wide-winged birds were making cleanly shapes. John Greggins went on, the wander-song lilting itself:—

> I solemnly swear that the heart in me rises
>   As the wind rises up and the mists break below,
> When I think upon Carra and Gallen down from it,
>   The Bush of the Mile and the Plains of Mayo!

It was after Saint Bride's day. Indeed, it was the end of the month. This very day he could draw his pension if he presented himself at Crossgar postoffice. And Crossgar was only twenty miles ahead. John Greggins set off on his journey.

He went into many a house to redden his pipe and to talk with the people. His soul gave greeting to the big roan horses that were pulling the carts on the mountain road. At last he came to Molloy's, a notable house of refreshment, within an ass's gallop of the town of Crossgar.

John Greggins went in, placed himself near the hostess and took his bread and butter and his glass. At the cross-counter there was an isolated individual who was making a feast of a tumbler of porter.

"It will be a good season for lambs," John Greggins announced.

The individual at the upper counter peered around. He was a beggar, but he had an eleemosynary look never affected by the poor men of that part. He was blind by a dramatic convention.

"It won't be a good season for lambs" he said, with a lift in his cringing voice. "It won't be a good season for lambs. The frost will come, and the young lambs will die in the field."

John Greggins felt called upon to justify his optimism. "I'm not depending upon lambs," he said: "I can go into the town of Crossgar now and draw my little pension."

"And what have you the little pension from, may I ask?" said the beggar.

"I have my pension from the Government," said John. The beggar turned back to the counter and sipped the dregs of his glass. Meagre was the bag that hung across his back, a bag that would never stand upright. He spoke to Mrs. Molloy: "This poor man won't hear the unlucky word from me," he said.

"And why should there be an unlucky word for the decent man?" asked Mrs. Molloy.

"Stocks are down, ma'am," said the beggar. "Sure, you saw that yourself in the paper. The Government are at a great expense over a war, and I doubt if they'll keep up the pensions." He shuffled towards the door, but turned back to John. "I'm greatly afeared, my good man, that your pension days are over," he said. "Stocks are down." He went out, and for John Greggins it was as if he had drawn a damp cloth across the sun and had shaken the drizzling rain out of his bag.

"Who is that man?" asked John.

"He's a poor man, but he's a very knowledgable man," said the widow. "There's truth in what he said. I saw in the paper to-day that stocks were down."

"I think I'll make haste and get to the letter office. There's no harm in getting ahead of bad news," said John Greggins.

The distance between Molloy's and the town of Crossgar was covered by a hurried march. The town was emptied—vacated, at it seemed to John Greggins's mind. He called to a boy who was minding an ass and cart, and asked to be informed of the way to the letter-office.

"Is it the letter-office that you want?" the boy asked in return.

"Ay, the letter-office," said John.

"It's the last house on the west side of the street," said the boy.

John Greggins crossed over to the west side, and headed down the street. He turned to the last house, and was confronted by a man who had his elbows along the top of the half-door. He presented a bald and massive head, and the appearance and reality of the hunched back.

"Is this the letter-office?" said John.

"The Academy of Correspondence," replied the man in a deep voice.

"And what beside that?"

"The Academy of Correspondence and the Depôt of Polite Letter-Writing."

"And has it anything to do with the payment of pensions?"

The Academy does not fulfil the functions of a post

office," said the hunchback. He opened the door and came out to John. "The Government Post Office is in the street abruting this," he said, indicating the place. "Remember the Academy of Correspondence. I am Dermott Mac Gilla Naeve, and my caligraphic skill is at your disposal."

"I'm obliged to you," said John, and without another word, gesture, or turning, he made for the post office. The scrutiny of his warrant gave John a few minutes' anxiety. The money was tendered him, however, and then the warrant was stamped and handed back. "Now, ma'am," said John, "I want to ask you a question. Will I be able to draw another draft of this pension at the end of the next quarter?" "Certainly," said the post-mistress, "or we'll have it sent to your address." "I heard the Government were in some hobble about money, and I thought maybe that they couldn't spare this. I'm obliged to them," said John. He stood still in the shop, meditating how he might express his gratitude to the Government. Then into his quickened brain came the thought of the Depôt of Polite Letter-Writing. He went across the street, and found the scribe before his door. "I want you to indite a letter for me," said John. Dermott Mac Gilla Naeve motioned him into the study. "This will be a particular letter. I want you to write to the Government headquarters." "I'll be glad of an outline of your case." "Well, it's like this," said John Greggins, and thereupon he set forth his relations to the State, and he elaborated his sense of obligation. To Dermott Mac Gilla Naeve this was material for artistic composition. He sat before the table, deep lines upon his great brow, and, after a while of labor and suspense, he produced the following:—

> Most Honorable Sirs,—An Epistle from the Humble hand of one who desires to express his Obligation to your Magnanimity. The years of my Service are amply compensated by the Recompense which your Benevolence has bestowed, and your Bounty together with the Paucity of my Vocabulary render an adequate Expression of my Gratitude impossible. To proceed without Pro-

lixity. I return due Thanks for this and former Favors, and with the deepest Veneration and Submission, I subscribe myself. Yours to command.

John Greggins.

This was the composition which the scribe read to John Greggins. "It's powerful," was the comment made by his client. "My honorarium is one shilling," said Dermott Mac Gilla Naeve. "And more would not be begrudged you," said John Greggins. John's eyes went down the sheet, and answering words rose to his brain. "The Statement of my case surpasses Pecuniary Expenditure. Fit an envelope for it now, and address it to the Paymaster of the Imperial Army." Dermott Mac Gilla Naeve took up the pen and achieved an elaborately decorated superscription. He received the honorarium, and conducted John out of the Academy of Correspondence. Like one in whom the inner flame has been lit, John Greggins trod the street. It was as though an order had been presented to his soul, conferring on it the pride of articulation. Into the blaze of the sunset he walked, and he stood upon the bridge that knit the town with the width of the world. The mountains were illuminated, the river was richly flowing, and the bridge gave one the pride of human handiwork.

There were idlers on the bridge; some grouped at the parapet, and some playing pitch and toss in the middle. They seemed companions fit for John's high mood. He turned to them and said, "I gaze upon this flowing stream, and I acknowledge that never before or since, in this or any other country, kingdom, or climate, have I beheld a scene of such surpassing magnificence." The men, who had been absorbed in the game, straightened themselves up and regarded John. "Behold the bridge," he proceeded: "think of them that in the old, ancient days raised it in majesty and in glory to be a pattern and a credit to their posterity." Then said one of the idlers, "This is a fellow out of Munster who thinks we are still in Reading-made-easy." And another said with palpable irony,

"Wouldn't you stand all night with your bare feet in the snow, to listen to him?" The tossed coin fell at John's feet; a gamester came forward to pick it up, and he said as he stooped, "It is easy knowing that before this the fellow never saw anything but the inside walls of a poorhouse." His head was within tempting distance, and John gave it a knock with the short end of his stick. The mêlée that followed was conspicuous to the police. To relieve the tedium of the evening, they sallied forth, and the one who was not aware of the way of escape fell into their hands. "We will put this down as a case of incitement," said the sergeant. "You may do that," said the young police-man, "for I saw him addressing the crowd and making very fierce gestures." There and then they decided to give John the cells for the night.

In the forenoon of the next day John Greggins took the road homeward. Silence was upon him like unto the silence beyond the trees and hedges, in the land of stones and shadows, where the very crows are lonely.

The PEACOCKS of BARON'S HALL

"THERE IS SOMETHING in the lease that I copied which sur-
prises me," said the Lawyer's Clerk, "it seems that
anyone who takes over Baron's Hall has to keep Peacocks—not
any Peacocks, but the Peacocks that are hatched out in the
place. I have been through the grounds and have seen the
Peacocks there—Peacocks that are so wild that they roost in the
trees—but I never knew before that the owner of Baron's Hall
has to keep them according to lease." As he talked about the
Peacocks and the lease old Simon the Huntsman came out of
the gate of Baron's Hall with his two old hounds beside him;
Kevin called to him, and asked about the Peacocks that were
now crying about the Hall. And this was the tale the old
Huntsman told:

"This stock of Peacocks has been about the Hall for a
hundred years and more. Long ago the estate which was a
great estate then was owned by one whom the people called
The Little Baron. He was only the size of a child of a dozen
years, and he had a sister, Lady Sabrina, who was the same
size as he. They were so small, so handsome, and so finely
behaved that much was made of them wherever they went.
They were in France once and King Louis brought the pair of
them to stay in his palace, and when they were leaving, the
King or one of his ladies, gave them a Peacock and a Peahen.

So the Little Baron and his sister came back to Ireland with the fowl, and they took up their residence in the place that was their father's, in Baron's Hall, which was newly built then, and the Peacock and the Peahen walked upon the lawn, and in a while a clutch of eggs was laid and hatched out and there were Peafowl in numbers parading before the Court.

"That was a long time ago, and the house and lawn were not as they are now, all untidiness and disrepair. It was a very stately place then, and the original Peacock and Peahen need not have missed the King of France's gardens. The Little Baron and his sister loved to walk where the Peacocks paraded, he in his gold-braided coat with a little sword by his side, and she in her flounces of silks and satins. A picture that is in the gallery shows them walking like that with the Peacocks spreading out their tails for the pair. It was a long time ago, as I have said, and things have changed, and some things have changed for the better. People who kept to the Catholic religion had no right to anything in those days. Well, the Little Baron and his sister belonged to that religion."

"And in consequence," said the Lawyer's Clerk, "the law did not presume that they owned anything or that they even existed."

"Something like that," said old Simon. "The Little Baron and his sister owned nothing in law. Though everyone acknowledged that he owned all his father had owned the law did not agree. He had no right to possession of anything at all. But his uncles who were not of his religion had the name of owning the estate; it was to them that all rents were paid; it was in their names that everything was bought and sold.

"Well, one day when the Little Baron was walking with Lady Sabrina along where the Peacocks were, their two uncles came to them in their big, heavy riding-boots, their riding-whips in their hands. And as soon as she saw them near her Lady Sabrina drew her arm out of her little brother's arm, and turned to go into the house. Then said brother John or brother Thomas very roughly, 'Enough of such behavior! You must treat us as gentlemen and relatives when we come to visit you!'

" 'Nothing,' said she, 'will ever make me acknowledge the presence of men who changed their religion for gain.' And saying this she walked into the house. She talked like this because she thought of nothing else but her piety. It wasn't the same with her brother—he thought of the grand house he was born in, of the pictures that were in the gallery and of the music that was played for him, and of the Peacocks that paraded where he walked. 'Yes,' cried one of the uncles when Lady Sabrina, drawing up her flounces went away from the sight of them, 'Yes. But what about these?' And one held up a bag of gold and the other a bag of silver that they carried. 'Here are the rents that your tenants have paid over to us. And if we were not there to receive it in our own names, where would this money go to? Not to where it is going now—into your steward's counting-house. If the government were not willing to suppose that we are the owners of all that is here, your servants could walk off with your silver and your pictures, your horses and your coaches, and there would be no one to stop them, for you have no title to anything here. Even these Peacocks on the lawn are not yours in the eyes of the law.'

" 'We know that,' said the Little Baron, 'and Lady Sabrina and myself live under the protection of the honor of you two. We are in your debt and greatly in your debt, and it is fortunate for us that our father's brothers were not averse to changing their father's religion.'

" 'It would have been to Hell or Connaught for you if we were,' said the brother who was the roughest of the two.

" 'Not so harshly, Thomas,' said the other.

" 'It is as well for those who live in Baron's Hall, who have the horses and the coaches and the servants, to know that if we wanted to, we and our children could have all this. The estate is ours in the eyes of the law, and all we have to do is to come here and take the benefit of it.'

" 'Yes, but men whose fathers were brought up in this house couldn't think of doing such a thing,' said the Little Baron.

" 'And we needn't talk about such things,' said brother

John. 'Only there will have to be consideration shown to us when we come here. We mustn't be treated as if we were some trooper's sons who have come upon some service to your Lordship. Well, come into the counting-house now and get your Steward to pass on the gold and silver we have brought you.'

"They went into the counting-house, his two uncles and the Little Baron, and the gold and silver was sorted, and the Steward entered the sum of it and went through his books to see if it made a balance. Then the Little Baron had his uncles sit down to dinner with him.

"But Lady Sabrina did not come to the table, and when brother John and brother Thomas muttered about this, her brother begged them to excuse her; they knew, he said, that she was pious, and this was the hour, he said, that she went into the chapel. But the uncles did not excuse her; they knew that she would not sit at table with them.

"After dinner brother John and brother Thomas smoked their pipes beside the chimney of the great hall and then made ready to ride to their homes. The Little Baron was not there to see them off. And as they were in their saddles the Steward came up to tell them that there was shortage in the money they had handed him and to blame them for it. This, added to the anger that brother John and brother Thomas already felt. They had faithfully brought all that had been given them in rents and here was a servant of the house that their father was born in checking them in this way. They turned upon him and ordered him to bring his master to where they were. But he would not do this: his Lordship, said the Steward, was in his gallery looking at the pictures of vales and groves in France and Italy, and no one was permitted to disturb him. He would report the shortage in the money to him, and that was all he could do about it. He kept on talking about his accounts, but brother John and brother Thomas lashed their horses and galloped down the avenue.

"And when they came to a rise of ground they halted

their horses and looked back towards Baron's Hall and saw a little man and a little woman walking on the lawn with Peacocks parading before them, and each said to the other that it was a shame that that great estate should yield benefit to a pair who thought only about pictures and peacocks and chapel-going. For a long time they sat upon their horses and looked over all the properties that they had title to—the fields of barley, oats, and rye with men reaping in them and women lifting up the sheaves, the woods filled with fine timber, the pastures with cattle and horses grazing on them, and then the lake with the fishermen's boats upon it. For the first time in their years of guardianship they begrudged these possessions to the Little Baron and became greedy for some of them.

"From that day brother John and brother Thomas began to think of their own advantage as against the Little Baron's. They lost the feeling that the great house their father had come out of should have all their loyalty and all their duty. They thought of the pair who lived there as odd little strangers who were always making claims upon them, always holding them at fault. They began to put to their own use part of the rents that came into their hands for the Little Baron. And when the Steward demanded an accounting from them they threw him into the bed of nettles outside his counting-house and rode away. Then they made great outlays with the money paid to them for the Lord in Baron's Hall: brother John bought a herd of fine cattle for his pasture, and brother Thomas bought the best of racers and hunters for his stables. A time came when they brought no money at all into the counting-house. Their cheating went on and the years went by. And brother John and brother Thomas, knowing they had dishonored their name, spent days in drinking and nights in gambling. They took the Little Baron's horses out of his stables, and they put their own fishermen upon his lake.

"They needed more and more money. Then there came an officer from England who wanted timber for the King's ships, and he offered them a thousand pounds for the woods that were around Baron's Hall. The brothers took the money and sent men to cut the trees and cart the timber away. The Little Baron was upon the lawn with his sister, and the Peacocks, now become a great flock, were parading before him, when the news was brought to him that the woods were being cut down. He and Lady Sabrina mounted their ponies and rode to where the axes were sounding. Many fine trees were already on the ground. Standing up in his stirrups the Little Baron ordered the wood-cutters to stop, and they, knowing what rights he had there, let the axes lie. But his uncles came forward and told the men to take their orders from those who had title to the woods, and told him that whether he liked it or not the woods would come down. The little man upon the pony denounced them for their faithlessness, and they turned from him as from an ungovernable child and bade the men who were near it to chop the branches off a tree that had fallen down sometime before.

"Its trunk lay over a wall that its fall had broken down and its roots were above a pit they had been dragged out of. These roots with the clay on them stood up like a mound and in a hollow amongst them a wren had built her nest. Young ones were in it; they were nearly ready to fly, and the mother, frightened at the sound and the shaking of the earth where her nest was, flew to them and away from them and back to them again. The cutting off of the branches would make the butt of the tree settle back into the pit again and crush the nest and the birds. Lady Sabrina saw this and she asked that the tree be left as it was until the wrens flew away. But the uncles would not have the men stop; there was nothing else for them to do with the light axes they had, and they must keep on working for their penny a day. The branches were cut off, the butt of the tree was slipped down when the little lady sprang into the pit and tore the nest out of its hollow. But what could she do with it? She left it on the ground and sitting down beside it broke into crying. The wren passed under her hand into and out of the nest.

"Then her brother took her hand and led her away. The two little people walked beside the ponies that the grooms led back to the Hall, and the men were ordered to bend their backs to the work.

"When he went home the Little Baron sat down and wrote letters to the gentlemen of the county informing them of his uncles' behavior. Many of the gentlemen refused to speak to or to recognize brother John or brother Thomas after that. But this was no help to the Little Baron's cause. For as the finer gentlemen fell away from them, the gentlemen whose rebuke might have mattered to them, the uncles took up more and more with men who coming from menial ranks had profited by the overturn of the old nobility. These men as they sat with brother John and brother Thomas, and drank with them or played cards with them, laughed at them for not taking possession of Baron's Hall and all that was in it and around it.

"Then, after a night at the gaming-table, with their clothes disordered and their faces heavy, his two uncles rode up to the front of the Little Baron's house and sent in a message that they were bringing the High Sheriff to visit him. They tramped up the stairway and they went into the room where the Little Baron was lying on his wide bed. The High Sheriff told him that the owners of Baron's Hall were about to take possession of it and of the whole of the estate. It must have been that the Little Baron had expected some such visitation, for he raised himself in his bed and said to them very coolly, 'Who said that I am not as well able to change my religion as others of my family?' And when he said that the heavy faces of brother John and brother Thomas became white and they drew away to talk together. For if he changed his religion, he would gain title to his possessions and his uncles would be cast off from his estate. 'Who said I could not change my religion like others of my family?' They hard him say the words over again to the High Sheriff, and they went out of the room and waited before the door. 'You have three days to come to me and take the test that will show you have come over to the King's religion,' the High Sheriff said. 'Three days—that is very well,' said the Little Baron, and he rose from his bed and dressed himself, and to be courteous to the High Sheriff who was himself a lord's son, he took him through the gallery and showed him his pictures of vales in France and groves in Italy. And by the time he brought the High Sheriff to the doorway, brother John and brother Thomas had ridden away.

"That evening they sat by their chimney, strong drink beside them, thinking they had been ill-counseled to go as far as they had gone. For if the Lord of Baron's Hall changed his religion, in spite of his sister's prayers, he would have title to his estate and the law would be with him. They would have nothing then—they would be men without place or fortune. Moreover, the Little Baron might be able to bring them to trial for some of the heedless things they had done, and make them fly the country, or see the inside of a prison. In three days they might,—they would be, they thought—at the mercy of the Little Baron.

"And he saw the sunlight on the turrets of his stately house and on the woods that were still around it, and he saw his Peacocks parading upon the lawn, and he thought that the only life that could give him pleasure and content was here, and that if he gave it up he would be mournful and complaining for the rest of his days—he would grow old as a feeble and banished creature. His sister prayed in the chapel that he might not forsake his religion, but he knew that the belief that made her pray so fervently was not in him. He had only to say that this belief was no longer his and he would have riches and the secure life that he and his sister needed more than any other man and woman. And the men who had humbled and tormented him would be at his mercy. He thought of all this, walking up and down there, and then with the firm tread of a man who has a right to carry a sword he went to where his sister was kneeling. 'What have you come to say to me?' she asked, raising up her little figure to stand beside his little figure. 'We belong,' said he, 'to the nobility of the Gael and the

Sean-ghaill, to the MacMahons and the Fitz-urses, and it is not for us to change our creed for riches and security. I who am rightfully the heir to that name and this place can say nothing else.' He gave his arm to his sister then, and they went upstairs and downstairs telling the servants that the house would be in their possession for only a while longer; then one went into her chapel and the other into his gallery, and they prepared for the leave-taking that had to be.

"When the High Sheriff came he found them watching their Peacocks upon the lawn. The little Baron led him into the house: the test that might be offered him, he said, he could not take. Then he had his Steward deliver to the High Sheriff all the papers that had to do with the family and the estate, and he gave his arm to his sister, and the two walked down the avenue of elm trees, while the servants who had been forbidden to make any clamor stood to watch them, and one pulled at the bell that was in the yard, and it rang very mournfully.

"Brother John and brother Thomas were outside the gate; they stood aside as the pair passed them. One and then another of the Peacocks cried. 'Do not scatter my Peacocks,' said the Little Baron to brother John. And the man made a sign of promise.

"The Little Baron and Lady Sabrina went to live in a lodge that was on a hill above this place; it had a sort of turret, and every day he and his sister would mount up and look across the wall and upon the lawn of Baron's Hall. They could see the Peacocks there and they would spend a long time watching them, and as they watched them they would remind each other of the Court of the King of France, and of the fountains and gardens and the stately life that was there. Their uncles with their families had taken possession of Baron's Hall, and the place was losing its stately appearance. More and more of the trees were cut down; the gardens became wilder and the lawn grew rougher. The lovely things that were within the house were taken away—brother John sold the pictures of vales in France and groves in Italy to give a dowry to his

daughter. But he would not have the flock of Peacocks scattered—they went upon the lawn, more and more of them.

"The uncles died, and the son of one of them came into
the ownership of Baron's Hall. This man, too, let the Peacocks
remain unmolested. But the wildness they grew up in lessened
the broods—the weasels got many of the young ones. The gold
lace raveled off the Little Baron's coat, and the silks and satins
that went into the flounces of his sister's dresses wore out.
They became so poor that often-times there was no candle to
light their chamber in the winter nights. But withal they remained a stately pair, and they would never take anything
from the Lord of Baron's Hall.

"They died in the lodge there, one going soon after the
other. The Little Baron dying first was buried in the grounds of
Baron's Hall. His sister asked that she be buried beside him,
and the ground was consecrated for her burial. I can show you
where the graves are—there where there are three dark yew
trees. Things have changed since they were buried there, and
Baron's Hall is no more than a ruin now. But the Peacocks are
still there, and, as the people will tell you, there is never a
season when a wren may not be seen fluttering about the
ground where the dark yew trees are. Many owners of the Hall
have come and gone since, but all of them left it in their wills
that the Peacocks were not to be banished. Aye, and when the
last of the family leased the place it was stipulated that the
Peacocks were to be kept."

"I copied that clause out," said the Lawyer's Clerk. "I was
much surprised by it."

"At some time of the year," said the old Huntsman, "the
Peacocks fly up into the branches of the yew trees and they can
be heard crying all together."

The SLOPES of TARA

A YOUNG CROW perched on a branch outside, barked insistently into a human habitation. Perhaps the internal conditions aroused the young crow's indignation. There were damp places on the floor where the rain came through the thatch; in one corner there was a bed with a ragged, miscellaneous covering. The room was filled with smoke, and the occupant was eating his breakfast off the top of a chest. He was seated on a box.

After a while the articulation of the crow took his interest, and he turned on the bird an eye that was remarkably like its own—a small, blue, penetrating eye. He finished his breakfast, put a cap on, and for a while surveyed the world from his doorway.

Before him were the lifeless grazing tracts of the County Meath. Formerly there had been a garden before the house that he was now the sole occupant of, and a cherry tree still growing showed that the place had once its grace and its cultivation. But the garden was gone back to the wild, and the house was an unsightly ruin. The man at the door was short of figure, and ragged of garb. His gaze was restless, and his quick, ever-moving glances reminded one of the looks of nature's smaller creatures, the rabbits and the squirrels. The man's mind also had gone back from discipline. He looked rather ruffianly, but there was humour in his face, quick judgment, and some practical wisdom. His cheek-bones were high, and his forehead projected, making a type that as some people think, shows a strong imagination, joined to an active and sanguine temperament.

The tumble-down house was solitary. Once the district was inhabited, but the place had been cleared of men and women, and had been given over to cattle. The man at the door was a survival from a vanished population. He was known by the name of Shaun, and he had employment on one of the grazing-tracts. Now, closing his door, he went off on his day's vocation.

Near his path a shoot of briar raised itself in the air. It was fresh, slender, and green. Shaun regarded it, and spoke out of his constant meditation. "The young girl is like the shoot of briar," he said, "for a while she's free and lightsome, and in another while she's without freshness and near enough to the ground." He picked up his stick and rambled away.

He worked to strengthen a fence, and then he brought a crowd of young cattle into a far pasture. Steadily they went through the grass where the pageant of sun, cloud, and shadow crossed the fields. He lay on the ground and gave his mind to a familiar romance.

Far away there was a rocky rise with some structure upon it. The legend of the place was part of Shawn's dream. The walls there were raised for the pleasure of a woman. A man had sworn that his bride would have a turret out of which she could watch the ships on the seas of Ireland. The ravens built in the tower now, he knew, but he did not moralise on this.

His delight was in the splendour and success of that man who had brought the woman there. No woman who kissed his mouth could ever take the kiss of another man—no other kiss but Farnie's kiss could she take. And Farnie was born to no estate although he had the spirit and the manner of a noble. He could win any woman, for he had "a diplume for coortin'." First there came to him a woman who had two score townlands. Then Farnie had blood-horses under him, and hounds to follow, and his own lands to ride across. The wife who had brought him these riches died, but Farnie was not left long to himself. A woman took his fancy and she had Cromwell's spoils for her dowry. Her brother would keep Farnie away, but one night he brought his horse under her window, and she came down to him, and they rode away together. He got five-score town-lands with that woman. Now Farnie had seven-score town-lands, and all that he willed he could do, and all that he longed for he could possess. And then when the second woman died Farnie's fancy was taken by another. She was young, a girl just, and she had no riches, but she had a beauty like the beauty that went out of Ireland when the foreigners came in. And it was to pleasure her that Farnie built the turret that Shaun looked towards now. He mixed the mortar with the bullock's blood and new milk, so that the walls might stand for a thousand years. But the woman never climbed the stair within, and the couple never slept inside the walls.

And now the cattle grazed upon the slopes of Tara. Furze bushes grew upon the mounds that marked the Banqueting Hall of the Kings, putting above the green their heaps of golden blossoms. There once the chiefs of the Fianna and the nobles of the Royal House feasted to the espousal of Grania, the King's daughter, and Fionn, the great captain. Grania drugged the ale, and while the elders slept she offered herself for wife to each of the young men who were most spoken of— to Oscar, to Coalite, and at last, to the most expert and the most beautiful of them all—to Dermott O'Duibhne. Then away the pair went together, and for long the wild and waste places of Ireland hid them from the wrath of Fionn.

Over the fields grew the sadness of vanishing light. Shaun stole away from the farmhouse where he had been given a meal. He took the road to the town, for he liked to draw away from the silence and the shadow, and his soul was lonely for some coloured and wonderful experience. Near the town he encountered part of a returning hunt. He saw a few silent people on horseback, and then he was surrounded by a silent-footed pack. He shrank from the dogs, and the silent, stealthy forms slipping through the evening seemed like a terror that had missed him.

Outside the town there were men in groups, and Shaun went up and stood amongst them. Before, when he was in this town, he caught sight of a beauty, and he thought that they men here might have some tidings of her. They were unenlightened. They played cards and they made jokes about one another, and they talked to him mockingly. He had been talking to this one and that one, and to the whole company of them. But it suddenly came over him that he must preserve the secret that he had—the secret of the beauty that he had seen. He watched the game they played and was silent, and when the game was finished he went from the men and into the chapel.

There were few people in the chapel, and the candles on the altar were not yet lighted. Shaun remained near the door, and kept his eyes on the organ loft. The Sunday before he had heard a voice singing up there, and he had seen a face and figure between the lighted candles. There was a young girl there; her hair was brighter and softer than the candles' flame.

The rosary began and went on to the litany, but there was no music from the organ. The candles that had been lighted on the altar were quenched now, and the people began to leave, their devotions over. The tolling of the bell outside made Shaun restless. He went out and into the street. Then he shifted through the town, shy and curious. He watched a soldier go into a house where there was a dance, and then he waited to speak with a ballad-singer, who had "The Lament for Hugh Reynolds."—

> By the loving of a maid,
> One Catherine MacCabe,
> My life it is betrayed; she's a dear maid to me.
>
> And now my glass is run,
> And my hour it is come,

And I must die for love and the height of loyalty
  I thought it was no harm
  To embrace her in my arms,
And to take her from her parents; she's a dear maid to me.

He was being drawn to a place of friendliness, but for a long time the wild shyness of his nature kept him abroad. At last he found himself before the place that he was drawn to—a trim house at the outskirts of the town. Within, someone was playing on the violin. Shaun waited, and when the music stopped he knocked at the door. The door was opened readily, as though a visitor had been expected, and Nora Kavanagh, the friendly personage to whom Shaun was drawn, stood there. Nora said, "Shaun, come in." She was not one of Shaun's admirations, but her friendly spirit made him devoted to her. He said, "Miss Nora, I'm ashamed to go into your nice house." He said this although he wanted to meet with some friendliness that night. "You must come in, Shaun, I'm expecting someone else, but there's no one with me yet." She brought him within and made him sit down. Nora was neat and precise, rather like one of the friendly, witty nuns one often mets in Irish convents; she was friendly to the odd characters that were about the place; their sayings and doings made a comedy that was always diverting to her.

"I found a plant with a grand flower to it," said Shaun, "and I'd have brought it to you only I thought you'd like to see it growing." His gaze roved about the room. He saw the violin that Nora had left down, and he brought his eyes to her face. "I'll bring it to you, root and all," he said, "and maybe you'll play a tune for me." She took up the violin and began to play.

The music brought back to him the loneliness of the empty fields. There was a green rath with trees growing upon it. Somebody was playing for a dance. But nobody could dance to that tune. It would be such a dance as he had never seen— the music was calling people out of the rath. He saw one who came out. Her face was pale like a star in a lake, and her

beautiful hair swept about her. Others were coming out of the
darkness; they were mounted on fine horses . . .

The tune ended suddenly; a quick knock had come to the
door, and Nora went to open it. When she came in again she
had another with her. It was the girl of his vision, and Shaun
recovered his sense of actuality only when she turned away
from him. Maybe Farnie's last love was like her, a slender girl
with all her life in her face, and different from the full-blown
beauties that Farnie had gathered in his day.

She leaned forward in the chair Nora had given her, and
she regarded the dreamer with friendly interest. He became
shy and uneasy, because he saw himself as an unkempt creature. He rose up and sidled to the door. He refused to eat;
Nora, knowing that she might not press him, let him go. "I
saw you before, miss," he said to the girl as he was going out.
"I saw you before, but you were far away." Then he went, and
when she came back to the room with Nora, the girl felt somehow lonely after the strange little creature who had gone out.

As for Shaun, he went along the darkened road in a state
of mind that was half satisfaction, half bewilderment. Woman
had ceased to be an abstract creature, the ornament of the
story, the spoil of the strong hand. Between himself and the
beautiful growing girl he felt the hundred ties of race. He was
the servitor who drove the swine into the woods, and she was
the daughter of a prince, but still they were related, and her
beauty was part of his dream and his glory.

The music that Nora had played seemed to come to him
again as he crossed the fields. He heard a voice that called
"Shaun, Shaun!" He knew that he was under an enchantment,
for the fields that he knew so well now had no mark, no
boundary. A sudden wind rustled in the grass. Shaun
crouched down, and a company of riders drew towards him.
The heads of the riders were bare, but across their brows there
were thin bands of gold. The one who rode in front had on him
the green mantle of a King. A rider turned his face to Shaun
and cried out in a clear voice: "He has seen her, the man in the

grass has seen her." But the clear voice that Shaun heard did not arouse the one who wore the green mantle. With bowed head the King rode on.

Then Shaun took up a handful of grass and threw it across his shoulder. He saw the landmarks, and the way through the night to his cabin. He made his way across the silent fields.

PILGRIMAGE HOME

Is it as strong on the road as it is here?" It was the wind they were taking about. So a woman inside her door would speak to one whose day was spent on the road: it would bring before him the miles and miles he had come, the men or women he had seen, the effort he had to make to get to where he was. But he would only answer with a word because the road and "here" were so different. Then for a young man who was there the journey he was going on took in elements of struggle that made it more real and rousing. There would be more on his road than he had thought of. And so this young man (call him Brendan) went out of the inn that had been his furthest house so far. Boys trooped out of school; they rushed into the belfry of the church, and began pulling the bellrope. To the ding-dong Brendan went on. "Be it so," he thought, taking the bell-ringing for a sanction. "It will be a pilgrimage."

The wind was strong on the road, strong like an animal. He struggled against it all evening and came into a town where everything creaked. The next day was clear and windless. As the young man strayed through the place he was drawn into a workshop—a long shed with floor thick with shavings. The red body of a cart was center, two red wheels were against a bench; on benches and hanging from above were many kinds of implements. Here, with his own carving tool he worked on used and disused wood that the cart-maker gave him. It was worth while looking at what went on outside. There was a fair there: substance and beauty were in the animals—aye, and in the men, too: there and there and there was a man who had quality so marked that, like one in a fable, he stood for something noble, or abject, or prophetic. The young man spent a long afternoon shaping a piece of wood and looking on lumpish men with bullocks, gallant-looking men with horses, scraggy-looking men with asses, wild-looking men with droves of pigs.

Putting clean straw into the weathered thatch a little man was perched on the top of a white-washed cottage. When the young man spoke to him, he raised himself; he showed the way through a flat country, pointing with the tool he held. He named the towns and villages the young man would have to go through; their names sounded like a litany. A little man perched on a house-top pointed the way to him with an antiquated tool. The hedges fell away, the road became open, going through a brook. Under a vaporous sky men were working, cutting into black turf-banks. There was a rooty smell from the earth, a smoky smell from the houses. Sometimes he was asked into a house; goat's milk that had acrid taste, the taste of the hedgetops, was in the tea given him. These roadside houses were weather-stained; they were cheerless; turf had not been dried yet, and the fires on the hearth were of roots and whin-bushes. But the road was going through what looked better land. A white ass, a brown ass, a black ass were together in a field of reddish rushes where clumps of trees outspread to gather in the twilight.

A girl standing apart from the couples assembled on the roadside spoke to him, and he lingered with her. Then a fellow who appeared to be conducting the proceedings—he held a switch in his hand as a wand of office—came to where Brendan was talking to his newly made acquaintance. "In this part of the country we have to do a lot to pleasure the young women, and if Rose here wants you for a dance, to be sure

you'll have the franchise of the place." He added, "We're asking something for the musicianer," and Brendan handed him
coins for the flute-player, a hunchback lad who had an air of
lonesomeness about him. Then the young man went into the
roadside dance with the girl who had spoken to him. "Take her
under the small rib," the droll-looking fellow with the switch
advised. The music of the flute was wistful, but the couples
went round energetically, vociferously. Readily he entered into
the gripping, swinging game. "Lace the girl to you, man!" and
"Mary, you needn't look as if you were never handled before,"
were the comments that the master of ceremonies made to one
and another of the couples. Linking arms they made a circle,
danced round each other, took new partners, swung again
with the first partner. Then the young man was standing in the
obscurity of trees with Rose, his arm about her. They sat like
other couples on the bank. Rose had dark eyes, but her whole
expression was in her wide mouth, unrestful or displeased.
"Maybe you think the girls here are for ramblers the like of
you," she said. She put her hand against his mouth and
laughed at him. He wasn't her sort—that was in her smile and
gesture. But he would make her know her sort in him before
he went on his way. They stood up for the next dance. She was
the tallest, the most mature of the girls on the roadside. He
would keep possession of her. But her mind wasn't given to
him at all; she was looking towards a newcomer.

As soon as the dance was over she left him with a bare
excuse and went to this newcomer. Should he lounge with the
others in care-free attitude or go on his way? If he could do it
with spirit he would do either, but his spirit was gone. Then
the master of ceremonies, bent evidently on conciliating him,
came to him. He brought another girl along. "The *gaer-calleach*
here would like you to dance with her." When the music began
again the young man had another partner. Nonie was her
name; she was the *gaer-ceallach*, the youngster of the dance.
After the dance, he sat with her; feeling rebuffed, he resolved
to go his way after the next dance. But the music of the flute

was touching, and he and Nonie got closer to each other. She had pleasant brown eyes the full gaze of which he only got now and then, for she kept them averted. Still their look was well pleased as they stayed longer together. Why, she was the nicest girl on the roadside, and he was prepared to rate her above the ill-mannered Rose. "We have the blackest horse that anyone ever saw in the town," she told him, bringing out a secret pride. "If you're in the town tomorrow—you may be mayn't you?—you'll see how I'm able to hold him in." He said he would see her with the grand horse, he told her, and her brown eyes remained for a while unaverted. Then he knew he could not be there, and was sorry, but holding her, did not say this.

The fellow with the switch came to them. *"A cuisle,"* he said to Nonie, "the musicianer will give up on us unless we can get you to stay beside him. Not another bar will he play for us unless you keep him company. I don't know what his honor here will think of us for taking you away, but what will we do if the musicianer renagues on us?" Nonie was still at the docile stage; she did not know what demands might with propriety be made on her in such an assembly as she was in, and showing distress she went with the master of ceremonies. The young man might make no protest for he was on suffrance amongst these merry-makers. He was downcast and angry. As he stood watching the beginning of the dance in which there was no partner for him he heard whisperings behind the hedge. He knew they were between Rose and the fellow she had left him for. "You mustn't—there are sharp eyes around!" He went on his way. He passed Nonie beside the humpback musician. Then he heard her coming after him. She stood with him, held for a minute. "I don't mind a kiss," she said.

"Brothers and sisters come to see them in the after-years," a chance companion said to him as he rang the bell of the monastery, "and the monks don't say a word to them—not one word. They just make tokens with their fingers." A bearded and brown-robed brother went ahead carrying their portable belongings. This side of the monastery was public and secular; the way into the otherworldly sphere was through the postern-gate at the other side of the quadrangle.

The bearded and brown-clad man took a bunch of keys from his girdle and put the largest into a lock.

"Where did you come from?" he asked.

Surprised by this lapse from silence Brendan mentioned the place he had started from.

"And so you're from the Capital?" their conductor said to the other.

"Yes, Father."

"You needn't call me 'Father.' I'm only a lay-brother. You will hardly see the Fathers at all. This way now. Do you know River Street?"

"I do, your Reverence."

"Oh, you needn't call me 'Reverence.' Don't walk into the bush. Do you know Collins' in River Street?"

"The big public-house—saloon they call it?"

"The very same."

"Everybody knows Collins'."

"I was there. A bartender for twenty years. See that now! Nothing is impossible to Almighty God. We go up the steps fornenst you."

It was very evident to Brendan that his fellow-guest thought, and the lay-brother himself thought, that the translation from the bar to the monastery was no less than miraculous.

"Brother Christopher is my name in this place," the lay-brother said.

The chance companion who had prevailed upon him to become a guest at the monastery was as moody a man as Brendan had ever known. He would change from exaltation to depression and from depression to exaltation as he walked about the garden or went in and out of the building. The lay-brother was the center of his interest: he followed him whenever he appeared.

Brother Christopher wrote little devotional poems; he would repeat them to the pair when they went into the dairy with him, serving them with mugs of buttermilk as he did so. As they walked in the garden afterward the moody man would discant to Brendan on the happy life that the lay-brother had attained to. He had been able to give up the world; from the counter of the barroom he had come near to the cloister; he was able to make poems that assuredly availed to his salvation. But could he, the questioner, leave the world? And would he be accepted in the monastery? His life was worse than mundane, for he followed sluts, drabs, draggletails. His head was held in his hands, and he huddled on a seat of the Monastery garden when Brendan went through the gate. He would go into the dairy, he would take a mug of buttermilk from the ex-bartender, and he would listen to another of his devotional poems. And in a day or two he would go back to the life he had tried to remove himself from. Brendan got no salutation from him as he went out on the road. It was twilight. All the noise that came to him was the gabble of distant geese, the twitter of small birds, the noise of little streams, or, now and again, the startled cry of a black bird.

Flames with terrible haste were destroying a habitation. The people who stood before the house or who dashed about were disheveled—even those who had just come on the scene were disheveled. The walls stood solid: they were of stone; the roof was slated. It was a large house and it stood by itself at a crossroads. Smoke came through the windows that were high up and through a gap where there had been a door. There was the spectacle of fire within the frame of walls. A horse that had been got out of the stable panted and made hoarse breathings. The young man became one of the crowd before the burning house. No one was in it now, it was supposed. But with the frightfulness of an apparition a man was seen amidst the smoke of the top window, pleading, appealing, screaming. "He came in drunk, lay on the bed, and no one knew he was there," someone explained. There was no ladder; women tied their heavy shawls together and men held them as a break for his jump. But he could not get through the window. Men went through the door with dash but turned back staggering. "The stairs are stone, thank God," someone said. But none of the adventurers had been able to ascend it. Then a soldierly look-ing young man, a dampened coat about him, made a dash into the house. There were no words from the onlookers, only ejaculations and heavy breathings, and from the women "God deliver him!" The man who had gone up shouted from the window; men ventured through the door again; excitedly they delivered the man who had been pulled out of the room and toppled down the stairs to them. He was carried from the conflagration, and the rescuer, after everyone had wrung his hand, made his way to the road and walked on as if he had a distant place to reach. Brendan went after him. The rescuer turned to him with a laugh and said, "The man I pulled out is the biggest gombeen-man in the county; the people who cheered his rescue should have blasted him out of the place. They're all in his books and he never lets them know how much they owe him."

They kept together. As they went on, the soldierly young man (his name was Tibbot Burke) told Brendan what he was settling out to do. It was to kindle insurgency here and there. He would drill young men in the hope that later on arms could be procured for them. "These people have never seen their own sort carrying arms. We have come to accept the fact that we are a disarmed population. I want to show the people com-panies drilling. I'm going to drill a company on the lawn before one of the big houses. I'll have them march through the gate, up the avenue, across the demesne. I'll have the lads drill before the house so as to rid them of the oldtime uplook they have."

But that would be in a part of the county that Brendan's pilgrimage did not lead to. Meanwhile he saw the country in a new way as he listened to his soldierly companion: he saw the land as something to be reckoned with, felt out, allied with: the hillocks, the river, the wide bog, the square gray old keep, the long walls of a demesne, the fields cut up by hedges, took on an aspect of human tension: they could be plotted with men's intelligence and will.

The young man showed his companion a figure he was carving.

"What is he doing?"

"Leaning on a slane. He's a man working in a bog."

"The wood is dark—that gives a look of the bog."

"I'm going to hollow the cheeks. The trousers, slipped down, will show the belly hollow, too."

"Why do you do it that way?"

"It's my way of making you feel the emptiness around him."

"And so you are tramping about to see the people of the countryside—the characters, I should say?"

"Characters is the word. I'm going abroad to study. But first I want to understand the character in the people and the place I'm related to."

"You are making a pilgrimage, you could say."

"You have said what I thought. It is a pilgrimage."

"What trade do you follow?" a farmer asked the two young men. There had been a hiring-fair in the town, and the boys who bound themselves for a season's service had gone off with their patrons. An anxious looking farmer remained. He did not want to hire help for a whole season: he and his brothers could mind their own ridges. But he had contracted to send a cargo of potatoes to Liverpool, and he was bound to have them at the Sligo boat in a week's time. Now he stood urgently before the pair, the town's watering-trough beside them.

Tibbot said to Brendan, "It's worth our while to go with

him. When you've spaded his ridges you'll know what to do with a spalpeen's arms when you're carving them, and I'll be able to judge the temper of the men up in the hills." So they clasped the farmer's hands in the bargain, and he put token-money, a shilling, into their hands. He gave them a meal with a pint of porter each, and when he came back from the shop to the eating place he announced, "I'm bringing a side of bacon to feed you." He mounted his nag and started for the hills, the pair following him on foot.

The next morning they broke ground with the hirer and his brothers. They were men who regarded their hillside, not as pasture and tillage fields, but as a domain that had to be guarded from aliens. They went from their fields into their house as into a fortress, and they talked of places below as if they were in another continent. The six men struck into the ridges; there was heard the scuffling of clay and the clanking of loose stones that the spades struck against. They left ridges trampled and formless as they dug away. Crows hopped there, delving for the cut or dwarf potatoes that had been left in the ground. Boys with two-creeled asses came along and filled the baskets with the clay-encrusted tubers: under the clay was God's plenty. Spades flashed as they lifted from the black earth.

The patron would take up a potato and weigh it in his hand and challenge the spadesmen to say if they knew a piece of ground—a "bank" he called it—that produced so greatly what was so sound. "Mind what I tell you," he would shout to the two he had hired, "the biggest potatoes are not always bose!" The proverb was like a triumphing refrain to the scuffling and clanking of the spades. It was used to contradict a defeatest notion—that there was hollowness in the big ones. The men spading in various postures, the man exultantly handling what he had taken out of the ground, stayed as figures in the carver's memory. Then the ridges were all cleared; the potatoes stood in a regiment of sacks; carts lumbered away with them, and the four MacGoverns were left to think over that venture of theirs that every year made ships and the sea part of their countings. As for the pair that had come to them, they parted on the hill-ridge, taking opposite ways.

He was in the center of it before he recognized that the town that was the end of his pilgrimage, so like it was to other featureless market towns he had passed through. The cawing of rooks, the jangling of the chapel bell, the bellow of a bull, the sound of a sledge on an anvil, all these sounds coming through each other in a particular way were what made the place a known one. He used to come here with his mother and father as to a place they were known in. Now he could not bring himself to believe that nothing from those days was left, and he stood in the street expecting to be recognized and spoken to. The one who came up to him was an ancient crone: her feet were bare and dusty, her hair was tangled and fell over her eyes, her face was full of grudges. Some legends of his forebears' lives this dusty-footed old beggar knew and had brooded on, and if he assured her who he was she would mutter something out of it. But with a look into his face, with nothing said, she went away from him.

Dooard the place was named: it was a story-telling name: the High Tumulus. On the hill that shouldered the place there were ancient stones. But there was another relic of ancientry there, and at it he would finish his pilgrimage.

It was a stone cross with a circle. An arm and a section of the circle was broken; the shaft must have been broken, too; some local mason had reset it in its place. Around it, seated on the rude pediment the mason had given it were lazy-bodies of the town or paupers out of the poorhouse taking the air. They turned their heads to him as he went to the cross. "So you've come back?" one of them, a dim-eyed old man said.

"Could it be that the old fellow remembered him? "But do you know me?" Brendan asked.

"It's the price of an ounce of tobacco he wants to get out of you," said one who had his back to the cross.

The old fellow shook his head vigorously. "It's not, then. I know him out of his father and mother, and why wouldn't I give a welcome to a young man that's come back to his own?" And saying this he stalked away.

"Who is he?" Brendan asked, wondering if he had any recollection of the old fellow.

"He used to be the bell-ringer in the town," one of the lazy-bodies told him. "Jack Stirabout is the name he goes by."

Often his mother, laughing, had capped something said by bringing in Jack Stirabout. He had always thought of him as a proverbial or fabulous character. And there he was, making his way west, up the stonewalled way that went to the gray building that was the poorhouse. Then came a recollection of a bell-ringer on this street: the jangling of the handbell, Brendan had thought, was to announce their beautiful jaunting-car with the spanking horse that his father handled.

The lazy-bodies went away, and the young man had the cross to himself. The crowned figure in the center was still whole; panel above panel, back, front and sides, showed crowds of figures in relief. Or were they figures and patterns encrusted on stone that had long been sunken in the sea? They were as worn as the words in prayers the people said. But examining the panels he began to find meaning in the figures and to understand what was significant in the whole monument.

He placed it as it should be placed: in his mind it stood at its right height, a cross with a wide circle round its arms, the crowned and dying figure in the center, and that circle of stone, and the panels, front and sides, filled with figures. A cross has not a monumental shape: straight up and straight across it lacks fullness and solidarity. But the sculptor of a thousand years ago, by encircling the arms, made the cross of stone massive, a solid. The one who did this had lived in this place, seeing the stones upon the hill (known then for a kingly tomb), hearing the cawing of the rooks, seeing these lithe young men with their mountain ponies, seeing the beggar woman with her tangled hair and dusty feet as the straggler after some defeat.

He could see in the worn, the small, grotesque but lively figures that filled the different panels, that the sculptor had seen such people as he saw today, and had put them at their avocations. A man with a hammer, a man leading a beast. He would have carved Jack Stirabout ringing his bell. All the folk he saw here today could be set along the sides of the cross, enhancing the significance of the figure in the center—the man, his wife and child in their cart; the ballad-singer; the man driving pigs. And the circle conveyed that idea of return which was in the minds of the people here of a thousand years ago, which he had found expressed by them in various remains.

Around him all was disorderly. The pigs being driven by men with such a wild appearance emblemed disorder. No monument or building that would make people thoughtful when they looked at it was here. There was disorder since there was nothing to give an idea of order. But by setting up something that would show the people a shape, some order would be brought into their minds and some order into such a place as Dooard. With his hand resting against the stone circle he said to himself that order could be brought out of this disorder. He heard the rooks above; he heard the strokes of the smith's sledge. A chill that was like the feeling of iron came over his body as he recognized who should make the shapes that the people would recognize. Out of what was before him even now he would make such shapes.

CATHERINE MULAMPHY
and the MAN from the NORTH

My GRANDFATHER USED TO SAY that more extraordinary things happened in the hamlet of Coney than in any town or village, barony or bailiwick in the whole of Ireland. They were all red-headed people and lived in Coney; they married through each other, and their names were Mulamphy. Now when he wished to illustrate the manifestations of the extraordinary Coney spirit, my grandfather used to tell this story.

Mind you, I knew two of the people concerned, Martin Mulamphy and his wife Catherine. Martin remains on the out-skirts of my mind, but Catherine I remember very well. I met her one day on a mountain road; she was riding; her bare legs hung across the donkey and her red hair was loose upon her shoulders. Even after they were married, Martin would not let this red hair be put up. My grandfather used to say that no two beings were ever as fond of each other as Martin and Catherine Mulamphy. Every Christmas, after Mass, the pair would come into our house. They used to sit on the settle, and after some whiskey had been taken, they would sing together, "The first day of Christmas my true-love sent to me one gold ring, one turtle-dove, *and* a pear-tree." The song, with proportional in-crease in the number of gifts, went on to the twelfth day of Christmas. When it was finished the pair would mount the horse, Martin in front of Catherine, and ride pillion-ways off to their mountain hamlet.

After Christmas comes the fair of Cartron Markey. It takes place at the rise of the year, upon Saint Brighid's Day. Now, our Mulamphys had nothing to sell, but that did not stand in the way of their going to the fair. And for the grandeur of the thing Martin put a pewter chain across his waistcoat. He had no watch to attach to it, but he remedied that defect by taking the lid of a small canister, fastening it to the chain, and putting it into a pocket. Appearance was everything, and Martin Mulamphy gave himself the appearance of a man who could sport a watch and chain.

The pillion was put upon the garron and the pair rode off to Cartron Markey. They put up at Mulvihill's. It was early in the day, and there were only a few people in the shop. Mulvihill himself was behind the counter, and Martin stood and discoursed with him. Catherine sat on a barrel at the far end of the shop. A Connacht man was closing a bargain with a man of the Midlands. "I declare to God," said the Connachtman, "I would divide the gain. *Dar na Muce!* By the pigs, we are as friendly as if we were kissing each other." They were shaking hands when another man came into the shop.

He was an Ulsterman and a horse dealer—a big man with a platter-broad face that fell easily into a grin. "Men, dear," said he, "what are ye havin'? Fill the glasses again," said he to the man behind the counter. "I've a heart as soun' as a prize cabbage."

"Is that so?" said Catherine from where she sat on the barrel, "and is there many in the fair that knows that?"

"Ma'am," said the Ulsterman, "I'd like to be talking wi' ye. Ye look like a fine woman."

"I was intended to be a fine woman," said Catherine, "and what is your name?"

"I'm Neil MacNeece," said the Ulsterman, "an' I'm a terrible great man. An' will ye take anything, ma'am?"

"A half glass of special," said Catherine.

"Tell us your story, honest man," said Martin, bringing back MacNeece's attention with a tap from a stick he picked up.

"Last year," said MacNeece, "I came into this fair with only three shillings in my pocket. All my money was lost in England. It was early in the mornin' when I came into your town and there was less than a dozen people in the place. There was a farmer with a horse for sale and I went up and spoke to him. 'How much do you want for the beast?' 'Eighty pound,' said he. 'Let me try him,' said I. I jumped up and galloped off, and that was the last the farmer saw of his horse."

"Do you tell us that?" said the man from the Midlands. The three men waited with glasses in their hands. MacNeece brought over the half of special to Catherine. "Good luck to you," said she.

"It's likely you have more to tell,' said the Connachtman.

"I have, and a lot more to tell," said MacNeece. "I came into your gran' town this mornin' an' found my farmer wi' another horse for sale. I stepped up and asked him his price. 'Eighty pound,' said he. 'Let me ride him to the end o' the town,' said I. 'Ye're a bit late, as Paddy said to the ghost,' said he, 'last year a villain asked me to let him try a horse, and I never saw him nor horse again.' 'An' would ye know the man?' said I. 'I would not. I saw him for no more than a minute.' 'I'll buy the horse without trial,' said I. 'Come into such a house and I'll hand ye eighty pound.' Well, I handed him eighty pound and he gave me a luck-penny. 'Would you be satisfied if ye got eighty pound for the horse ye lost last year?' 'I'd be more than satisfied.' 'Well, here's your eighty pound. It was me that took your horse. An' look,' says I, showing my pouch to my farmer, 'I made all that out o' your nag.' "

"You're an extraordinary wonderful man," said Catherine.

"Sowl, but ye're a gran' woman," said MacNeece.

"Do you like me?" said Catherine.

"Ma'am, I like you well," said MacNeece.

It was at this moment, as luck would have it, that the Connachtman asked Martin for the time of day. Martin whipped at the chain. Out flew what was attached to it. It rolled. No wheel of fortune ever rolled as that lid of canister rolled. It rolled behind the counter, the Connachtman pursuing it. It rolled from behind at the upper end of the counter and out upon the middle of the floor. Another man went after it there. It rolled behind the barrel on which Catherine was sitting. As it rolled between his legs MacNeece picked it up.

"And is that what he was going to give us the time of?" said the Connachtman.

"Sowls!" said MacNeece, holding the canister-lid between finger and thumb.

"I thought he had one watch at least," said the man of the Midlands.

"Ye thought wrong, like Paddy's pig," said MacNeece with a grin.

Then the Connachtman and the man of the Midlands went out. Martin took the canister-lid from MacNeece and threw it down on Mulvihill's counter. "Are you buying?" said he to MacNeece.

"The one thing I'd like to buy is the red-headed woman yonder."

"Do you make an offer?"

"Do ye own her, now?"

"It was me that put the ring on her finger." Catherine came over to the pair. "What would you give for me?" said she to MacNeece.

"I'd give all I have, ma'am," said MacNeece. "I would, in troth." He took a roll of notes out of the inside pocket of his great-coat and put them on the counter. There were twenty of them. Now there was something of the jackdaw and something of the magpie in Catherine's husband. He was acquisitive and he was vain. He had just put on a new belt. It was a red belt with blue stripes across it, and it had leathern pouches. The notes got inside one of the pouches. Then Martin Mulamphy would let himself be cut across rather than take one of them out.

"Give the man a luck-penny, Martin," said Catherine.

Martin took a crooked ha'penny out of his pocket and

passed it to MacNeece. "Will I be takin' ye to the North?" said MacNeece to Catherine.

"You must give me law," said Catherine.

"What law do you ask?"

"A year and a day."

"An' whaur will I find ye at the end of the year an' the day?"

"In Coney," said Catherine. "Mulamphy is the name. Come," said she to Martin, and then she went into the street. And all that her husband said to MacNeece was, "Good-bye to you, honest man."

They went down the street without a word between them, Catherine and Martin. At the corner there was for sale a cart of splendid appearance. The spokes and shafts were freshly painted red, and the body was of a shining blue. Martin priced the cart, and Catherine stood by and watched the proceedings. She had become the onlooker of Martin's motions and movements. The cart went to three pounds, and Martin paid with money out of the pouch on his belt. He put the garron under the yoke, and the pair went home in their new vehicle. But it wasn't like being on the pillion. There was silence between the pair for the length of the road.

Christmas came around, and Martin and Catherine came into our house. They sat down on the settle and took the refreshment provided. They sang together, "The first day of Christmas my true-love sent to me one gold ring, one turtle-dove, *and* a pear-tree." They went out together, and my grandfather watched them from the door. "Believe me," said my grandfather, "I would give that full bottle of whiskey to see Catherine and Martin Mulamphy riding pillion-ways again. Since they came by that cart I see a difference in their nature towards one another."

Martin had told him the episode of Cartron Markey, and my grandfather had given him this sage direction, "Whatever else he'll come for, believe you me, the man of the North will come back for his money. Leave the seventeen pounds in the pouch, roll up the belt, and let me have the keeping of it." Now, upon the next Saint Brighid's Day my grandfather was before the house clipping his hedge into the semblance of a lion, when a stranger strode up to him. "Where is Coney?" asked the man. My grandfather knew him at once for the man from the North. "Maybe you're looking for the people of the name of Mulamphy?" "I am," said the man, and he had a wide grin on. "Your name might be MacNeece?" "It is MacNeece," said the man. "We have heard of you," said my grandfather.

He put MacNeece on the way to the hamlet, but he neglected to tell him that everyone in Coney was named Mulamphy. He went into John's with the Two Chimneys, to Michael's with the Running Dog, and to Bartley's the Tailor. Nellie, the tailor's wife, didn't let him leave in a hurry. Well, between one house and another house, Neil MacNeece spent about half his day between doorstep and hob.

My grandfather was playing a game of cards with himself when he saw Catherine upon the road. She had a bundle, and my grandfather thought she was bringing his dinner to Martin. He was trimming a hedge for him that day, but my grandfather had not remembered this when he was speaking with MacNeece. "Good-morrow, Catherine," said my grandfather.

"Good-morrow," said Catherine. My grandfather thought her manner was not effusive at all.

"Your man will be glad of his dinner," said my grandfather.

"I'm not going to provide it," said Catherine.

"But where are you going, then?" said he.

"From the house that he brought me to," said she.

"The man that put the ring on your finger?" said my grandfather.

"There it's for him," said Catherine, throwing the ring— she was holding it in her hand all the time—in the dust of the road. Catherine went her way. My grandfather left his cards and walked up and down. Then he called to me and bid me bring Martin Mulamphy to that spot. "Martin, my poor fellow," said my grandfather, "there's your ring on the ground." Martin took up the ring. "It's Catherine's surely," he said. "I won't keep you in suspense, Martin," said my grandfather, "Catherine threw it there." Martin regarded the ring. "She wasn't great with me for a few days back," said he, "but why should she go off like that?" "With a bundle, Martin," said my grandfather, "as if she was going to work in Scotland or England." "But it's not the season for that," said Martin. "This is only Saint Brighid's Day. By the Cross of Cong," said he, shearing the top off a hedge with his billhook, "she's gone off with the man from the North."

"Don't say that, Martin," said my grandfather, "don't say that, and give me the billhook out of your hands. But I have to own," said he, when he got the billhook into his own hands, "that Neil MacNeece was round here this morning, and I gave him all directions for finding your place."

"Amn't I the misfortunate man," said Martin, "with my wife gone off with a black-mouthed man from the North?"

"The like never happened in this parish," said my grandfather, "and I'm loath to believe anything of the kind."

"It was a bargain," said Martin.

"Somehow I didn't see what you think in Neil MacNeece's eye, anyway, Martin. And Catherine went from this by herself."

"I'm very venomous," said Martin. "When I'm roused up I could puck my weight in fighting-cats. I'll let daylight through MacNeece if he was to have me hanged for it afterwards."

With that he dragged on his coat and made a run of about twenty yards. My grandfather called to him. "Martin," said he, "rash men will do rash deeds I know, but a man oughtn't to show himself to the world worse than his deed makes him. Don't let the name of money come into the dispute, Martin. Give back what you have belonging to him." My grandfather went into the house and brought out the belt. He handed it to

Martin Mulamphy. With the belt in his hand he started down the road. He was making for his mother-in-law's. He would borrow a horse and ride into Cartron Markey.

He came to the cross roads and went down by the plantation. Ahead of him he saw a man in a great-coat walking hard. It was Neil MacNeece. Martin caught up on him. "Och, Mister Mulamphy," said the big man, "I hope I see ye soun'."

"I'm sound enough," said Martin, "and I have the use of my hands. Would you try a few rounds with me?"

"Here, is it?"

"Here, on the road."

"Is fightin' your wish?"

"Aye, what have you to say again' it?"

"Nothing again' it. The spirits are that ruz in me that I'll do anything to oblige any man. Fightin', is it? Oh, very well, Mr. Mulamphy."

"Take the belt," said Martin, "your money's in it."

They went down the road a bit. When they came to a ground he knew Martin took up a position. He struck out. MacNeece sparred good-humouredly. Martin was certainly venomous. He manœuvred the fight till he got MacNeece on the ground that dipped to a rotten fence. He struck out; he got his adversary on the mouth and nostrils. Through the fence went MacNeece and into a slough of water. Then Martin turned on his heel and went up to his mother-in-law's.

Catherine's mother was at the door. "Wiat a while," said she, "and then go up to her."

"What? Is Catherine here?"

"She's in the room above."

When he opened the room-door he saw Catherine lying in bed. She turned angry eyes on him. "You're as mean as ditch-water," she said, "and I'm glad I saw you to say that to you."

"No matter how mean I may be I've done for the man you were going off with."

"The man I was going off with?" Catherine said. "Who are you talking about at all?"

"Neil MacNeece. I met him and fought him and left him lying in a snough at the Kesh of Keel. That's what your bachelor got this Saint Brighid's Day."

Catherine sat up in bed. "Martin, are you hurted?" she said. She came to him. "Martin, Martin, you're cut and battered. Did he hurt you, Martin? But why did you do badly by me? You said it was a gold ring. After wearing it five years I found you out in a lie. It's a brass ring, after all. Oh, it's badly you treated me! I'd have a right to go off with Neil MacNeece."

"Were you not going with him?"

"Sure, Martin. I clean forgot that this was Saint Brighid's Day. What did he do to you, Martin?"

"I gave him back his belt and fought it out."

"I didn't know he was this side of the world. But I own to you that it makes me proud that he came for me. You didn't give him his twenty pounds back—oh, no, you didn't, Martin, for you've a mean drop in you. I'll never wear that oul' brass ring again, and I'll make you give the rest of Neil MacNeece's money back to him."

She had just said the words when MacNeece's voice was heard below. She went down the stairs and saw him at the door. And she showed her presence of mind by the way she up and spoke to him. "Mr. MacNeece," said she, "isn't your call too soon? I thought we wouldn't see you for a year and a day?"

"But, ma'am," said he, "it's twins!"

"Oh!" said Catherine. He was shaking hands with her mother and telling about the event.

"Twins. Mrs. MacNeece, ma'am. Two days ago."

Martin was coming down behind them. Catherine turned to him. "It's seldom Mr. MacNeece is in these parts," said she to him, "and we must do our best to pleasure him. Leave everything aside and we'll go off for the day."

Martin put the horse under the cart. When everything was ready he came in and shook hands with MacNeece. Nothing was said about the previous encounter. They went off to Cartron Markey. They had all the fun of the fair. A tramp fiddler entertained them in the room, and MacNeece began to drink with him. But it turned out that the blind musician was pouring the whiskey into a tin behind his wallet so that he might have something after he left Mulvihill's. This unfair competition brought the horse-dealer under; MacNeece was left sleeping in the cart, and Catherine and Martin rode home pillion-ways. They came into our house on their way back. Just as if it had been Christmas, the pair, sitting together, sang of the ring, the turtle-dove, and the pear-tree.

The DEATH of the RICH MAN

I T WAS A ROAD as shelterless and as bare as any road in Munster. On one side there was a far-reaching bog, on the
other side little fields, cold with tracts of water. You faced the
Comeragh hills, bleak and treeless, with little streams across
them like threads of steel. There was a solitary figure on the
road, a woman with bare feet and ragged clothes. She was bent
and used a stick; but she carried herself swiftly, and had something of a challenge in her face. Her toothless mouth was
tightly closed, her chin protruded, wisps of hair fell about her
distrustful eyes. She was an isolated individual, and it would
be hard to communicate the sensations and facts that made up
her life.

Irish speakers would call the woman a "shuler." The
word is literally the same as "tramp," but it carries no anti-
social suggestion. None of the lonely cabins about would re-
fuse her hospitality; she would get shelter for the night in any
one of them—the sack of chaff beside the smouldering fire, the
share in the household bit. But though she slept by their fires
and ate their potatoes and salt, this woman was apart from
them, and apart from all those who lived in houses, who tilled
their fields, and reared up sons and daughters; she had been
moulded by unkind forces—the silence of the roads, the bit-
terness of the winds, the long hours of hunger. She moved
swiftly along the shelterless roads, muttering to herself, for the

appetite was complaining within her. There was on her way a
certain village, but before going through it she would give
herself a while of contentment. She took a short pipe out of her
pocket and sought the sheltered side of a bush. Then she drew
her feet under her clothes and sucked in the satisfaction of
tobacco.

You may be sure the shuler saw through the village,
though her gaze was across the road. Midway on the village
street there was a great house; it was two stories above the
cottages, and a story higher than the shops. It was set high
above its neighbours, but to many its height represented effort, ability, discipline. It was the house of Michael Gilsenin,
farmer, shopkeeper, local councillor. "Gilsenin, the Gombeen
man," the shuler muttered, and she spat out. Now the phrase
"Gombeen man" would signify a grasping peasant dealer, who
squeezed riches out of the poverty of his class, and few people
spoke of Michael Gilsenin as a Gombeen man; but his
townsmen and the peasants around would tell you that
Michael Gilsenin had the open hand for the poor, and that he
never denied them the bag of meal, nor the sack of seed-
potatoes; no, nor the few pounds that would bring a boy or girl
the prosperity of America. To the woman on the ditch Michael
Gilsenin was the very ermbodiment of worldly prosperity. It
was said, and the shuler exclaimed on Heaven at the thought,
that Michael's two daughters would receive dowries of a
thousand pounds each. Michael had furnished the new chapel
at a cost of five hundred pounds; he had bought recently a
great stock of horses and cattle; he had built sheds and stables
behind his shop. And Michael Gilsenin had created all his
good fortune by his own effort. The shuler wondered what bad
luck eternal justice would send on his household to balance
this prosperity. And in her backward-reaching mind, the
shuler could rake out only one thing to Michael's discredit.
This was his treatment of Thady, his elder brother. It was
Thady who had owned the cabin and the farm on which the
Gilsenins had begun their lives. Michael had reduced his
grasping and slow-witted brother to subordination, and he

had used his brother's inheritance to forward himself. In forwarding himself Michael had forwarded the family, Thady included, and now, instead of life in a cabin, Thady had a place in a great house. Michael was old now, the shuler mused, he was nearly as old as herself. It was well for those who would come after him. His daughters had dowries that made them the talk of the county, and his son would succeed to stock, farms, and shop. The shuler stretched out her neck and looked down the road and on to the village street. She saw the tall grey building, the house of stone with the slated roof and the many windows. And she saw a man hobbling out of the village. He had two sticks under him, for he was bent with the pains. The man was Thady Gilsenin, Michael's brother.

Thady Gilsenin was grudging and hard-fisted to the beggars, but he always stayed to have speech with them. His affinities were with these people of the roads. By his hardness, and meanness, by his isolation and his ailments, he was kin to the shuler and her like. She quenched the pipe, hid it under the clothes, and waited for Thady Gilsenin.

He stood before her, a grey figure leaning on two sticks. His hands were swollen with the pains, their joints were raised and shining.

"Well, ma'am," said Thady, "you're round this way again, I see."

"My coming won't be any loss to you, Thady Gilsenin," the shuler returned.

Thady turned round and looked back at the big house.

"And how is the decent man, your brother?" asked the shuler, "and how are his daughters, the fine growing girls?"

"His fine daughters are well enough," said Thady, turning around.

"There will be a great marriage here some day," said the shuler, "I'm living on the thought of that marriage."

"It's not marriage that's on our minds," Thady said, in a resigned way.

The shuler was quick to detect something in his tone.

"Is it death?" she asked.

"Ay, ma'am, death," said Thady. "Death comes to us all."

"And is it Michael that is likely to die?"

"Michael himself," said Thady.

This to the tramp was as news of revolution to men of desperate fortune. The death of Michael Gilsenin would be a revolution with spoils and without danger. She was thrilled with expectancy, and she said aloud: "O God, receive the prayers of the poor, and be merciful to Michael Gilsenin this day and this night! May angels watch over him! May he receive a portion of the bed of heaven! May he reign in splendour through eternity! Amen, amen, amen!" And crying out this she rose to her feet. "I'm going to his house," she said. "I'll go down on my knees and I'll pray for the soul of Michael Gilsenin, the man who was good to the poor." She went towards the village, striking her breast and muttering cries. Thady stood for a moment, looking after her; then he began to hobble forward on his two sticks. They were like a pair of old crows, hopping down the village, towards the house of Michael Gilsenin.

She could never have imagined such comforts and conveniences as she saw now in the chamber of the dying man. There was the bed, large enough to hold three people, with its stiff hanging and its stiff counterpane, its fine sheets, its blankets and quilt, its heap of soft pillows. There was the carpet warm under her own feet, and then the curtains to the window that shut out the noise and the glare. A small table with fruit and wine was by the bed, and a red lamp burnt perpetually before the image of the Sacred Heart, and so the wasting body and the awakening soul had their comfort and their solace. Michael's two daughters were in the room. They stood there broken and listless; they had just come out of the convent and this was their novitiate in grief. The shuler noted how rich was the stuff in their black dresses, and noted, too, their white hands, and the clever shape of their dresses. As for the dying man, she gave no heed to him after the first encounter. He was near his hour, and she had looked too often upon the coming of death.

They gave her a bed in the loft, and she lay that night above the stable that was back of the great house. She had warmed herself by the kitchen fire, and had taken her fill of tea, and now she smoked and mused, well satisfied with herself. "This night I'm better off than the man in the wide bed," she said to herself. "I'm better off than you this night, Michael Gilsenin, for all your lands and shops and well-dressed daughters. I'm better off than you this night, Michael Gilsenin, for all your stock and riches. Faith, I can hear your cattle stir in the sheds, and in a while you won't even hear the rain on the grass. You have children to come after you, Michael Gilsenin, but that's not much, after all, for they'll forget you when they've come from the burial. Ay, they will in troth. I've forgotten the man that lay beside me, and the child that I carried in my arms." She pulled a sack over her feet and knees and up to the waist, and sleep came to her on the straw. But she was awake and felt the tremor through the house, when Death came and took his dues. From then onward her sleep was broken, for people had come and horses were being brought out of the stable. Once old Thady came out, and the shuler heard him mutter about the loss in hay and oats.

When she came down to the yard she saw a well-dressed young man tending his horse. One of Michael's daughters came and stood with the young man, and the two talked earnestly together. The shuler knelt down on a flag and began sobbing and clapping her hands. She was working up to a paroxysm, but gradually, for she wanted to attract the attention of the pair without distressing them overmuch. The girl went indoors and the young man followed her. The shuler saw two empty bottles; they were worth a penny. She hid them under her dress and went into the house. She made her way to the front door, passing by many. People of importance were coming, and in such an assembly something surely would be gained. She stood by the street door and watched the great people come—priests, doctors, lawyers, shopkeepers, and councillors. She stood there like an old carrion bird. Her eyes were keen with greed, and her outstretched hand was shaking. She heard old Thady saying, "Now, thank God, we can be clear for the day of the fair. I was thinking that he would still be with us on the fair day, and we would have to close the shop, and that would be a great loss to us. Now we can have everything cleared off in time. God be good to Michael's soul."

DUBLIN

A DUBLIN DAY

PEOPLE USED TO ASK who he was. Mortimer O'Looney the poet, they would be told. He read papers at literary societies; his verse appeared in the Sunday edition of a daily paper. Once the Office of the King's Parks and Manor in which was incorporated the King's Retinne's Emoluments had claimed his presence—in fact he was Paymaster to the King's Fifes and Kettledrums—but on the abolition of that office he was presented with his liberty and an annuity of one hundred and four pounds while still a youngish man. He lived at the North Side of the city.

In the course of the day the feeling would go from him, but his morning's wakening was generally to a sense of power-lessness. The lamp stood with its shade awry; his clothes, from a peg at the back of the room door, hung like a strangled man; the papers on his table looked stale and the books in the shelves lifeless; the sun was in his room and the day yawned at him. On the morning of a certain summer day, however, he wakened to lie as complacent as a cat on a sunny wall. "This is no ghostly literary inspiration," he said to himself. "This is material good. This is money." He turned out of bed. The water he poured into the enameled basin, he felt, had some real relation to wells and streams. " 'Tis fatness instead of lean-ness, 'Tis beef instead of bread," said Mortimer. " 'Tis dinners, drinks, bills paid, self-assertion. 'Tis a break with an enfeebling round." A full-blown rose was in the glass of water; he took it with him downstairs.

Katie, his landlady's sister, had brought in breakfast and was putting on her hat in the room. He presented the rose. "Katie," he said, "'tis a long time since I gave you a present."

"It is, faith," said Katie.

"I'll give you a new belt."

"You're joking me," said his landlady's sister.

"I'm not. I've still a little property. I thought about it this morning. I remembered it in a dream."

"How much is the property worth, Mr. O'Looney?"

"Between fifty and seventy pounds. 'Tis a large double grave in the center of the cemetery. 'Tis my grandmother's grave. Only one side was ever used."

"And can you sell it?

"I'm the only one who has any claim on it. They'll probably offer me nearly a hundred pounds for it."

"I'm glad you're getting the money."

"You'll get the belt, Katie. How many inches? Thirty-six?"

"God forgive you! Twenty-six. With big clasps, mind."

"'Twill be all right," said Mortimer O'Looney. He went on with a breakfast that consisted of tea and toast. When he came to his second cup, he said:

"Katie, would you borrow five shillings from the landlady for me?"

"That will be fifteen and sixpence this month."

"'Twill be all right. I want to buy something before I draw my money." Katie went out and came back with the five shillings. Mortimer O'Looney took a cane from the hall and went out upon the top doorstep.

"Mind, with big clasps," said Katie.

"'Twill be all right," he answered. "This is Mortimer's day."

It was the sort of day that gives content to cripples and blind people, to old men and women, to strollers and idlers. Mortimer's way was through a little neglected park. The grass was long and wild; shadows crossed it, and the passing wind made a sound in it. He was pleased with the grass, with the shadows and the sound, and pleased that his soul was pleased with these things. And so he made his way into the outlying streets and then into the center of the city.

The Nelson Column was there. A thousand days he had passed it without concerning himself at all with it. But to-day the granite shaft seemed to lift itself to a higher height and into a bluer depth of the air. A pigeon flew up from the street and its flight failed before it gained the top. " 'Tis a gigantic stalk whose granite flower seeks the blue of the air," said his Genius to Mortimer O'Looney. The poet considered the column. It expressed the idea of height and liberation, or rather, the idea of liberation through height. "You should climb to the top of it," said his Genius to him. "I never thought of climbing it before." "This day has never occurred before," said his Genius. "It is provincial to mount Nelson's Pillar," said O'Looney. "But it is what a poet of the decadence would do," said his Genius. So he paid his three-pence and entered the cavern at the base of the shaft. He climbed the thousand steps inside the funnel, and emerged into the light of day.

It was liberation indeed. It was as if he were lifted above the crowd by a gigantic hand. He was in a clearer and more invigorating air. Over the roofs of the gray, huddling houses he looked and saw the encircling hills and the river touching the sea. He saw

"Sunlight on the Hill of Howth,
And sunlight on the Golden Spears,
And sunlight out on Dublin Bay."

and looking down he noted the colors of the fruit and flowers that women were selling below. He heard music up here. Of course no lark sang above the city, and the song of the caged lark could not reach him up here. But he heard a lark's song.

He heard it in his mind's ear. This was a theme for a poem—
the song of the lark that came to the one who climbed into the
clear spaces. As he stood there the poem came to him. He
heard rimes. He caught the beat of the rhythm. The poem fell
into stanzas, and, sitting with his back to the pedestal of the
statue, he began to write it down on the back of an envelope.
Below, citizens crossed the tesselated pavement—at least the
cobbles had a tesselated effect looked at from this height.

He had coffee and a cigarette; he went over his poem
putting it into semi-final shape. Then he stood out a certain
street corner rehearsing what he would say to his friends. "It's
curious that I've taken to writing verse again; I've just finished
a lyric, and I'm inclined to think that it's the best thing I've
done. I'm putting it into a book that I've had by me for the past
few years. Yes, I'll tell you the piece. Well, here it is." And once
again he repeated the poem to his own satisfaction. He would
have the chance of confiding the miracle to two or three fellows, for at this corner, at the mid-hour, one encountered the
bards.

Eimer MacMahon, with his deliberate effusiveness,
greeted him and remained in conversation with him. Mortimer
had worked up to a recital of the poem when Edmund Blake
appeared. Blake, coming over to them, made a motion as if he
had a rapier in his hand. "O'Looney," he said, "I've just put
you into a scandalous poem. Really I have nothing against
you—you are a blameless man, I know—but I had to use that
name of yours." Thereupon he repeated the most scandalous
of the quatrains. "You're further down," Blake said. "I have
you with the minor men." He went off, taking MacMahon with
him. Then another bard, Hubert Murtagh, appeared. A
thought occurred to O'Looney: Murtagh had the face of a fugi-
tive; no matter how long you were with him you only saw his
face in glimpses. Murtagh passed with a duck of his head.
"That fellow has no friendship," O'Looney said to himself, "he
must be a County Cork man." He remembered an epigram
some one had made about Hubert Murtagh. "Whenever I see

him I look out for the pigs." Really, Murtagh went down the
street as if he were driving invisible pigs.

And then he sighted Anthony Wade. This bard greeted
him with a hand held high. Anthony Wade crossed the street
like a man pacing tracts of delicate beach, his breast filled with
ozone. His hat was in one hand and he held a book of French
verse in the other.

"I've been trying," he said, "to get the word that de-
scribes the pull of those heavy horses that are still upon the
streets. I have just got it. But have you written anything?"

"I've just written a lyric."

"Come into the Corner Tavern and let me have it."

"I'll go in. But not to stay in the place. I've some business
to transact to-day."

"Don't talk of business while that sun is in that sky. I've
sworn to keep the daylight pure. Come along. A man with a
new lyric is bound to bring me luck."

In a few minutes they were in the Corner Tavern, seated
on high stools before the counter. O'Looney ordered vermuth.

"For finely tempered minds," said Anthony Wade, "there
is in a public-house an attractiveness which is only collaterally
related to the delight of imbibing liquors. That attractiveness is
connected with the idea of a symposium. In a way I prefer the
public-house to the *café*. No, I haven't been in Paris. I am going
next spring. But at this time of the year I psychometrize Paris. I
get the whole feeling of being there." He put the volume with
the lemon-colored covers on the counter and lighted a
cigarette.

O'Looney looked through the verse in the book.
"Verhaeren," he said. "But I don't like French poetry that's not
in even lines." Thereupon Anthony Wade began to expound
his theory of metrics. No man in Dublin could be more elo-
quent upon such a subject.

A dining-room adjoined the bar. Out of it came a waiter.
He presented a note to O'Looney. "Gentlemen, I have been an
unworthy listener to fragments of your conversation. Perhaps

one about to leave his native land may claim the privilege of the company of two of her poets." They went into the dining-room. A gentleman at a table bowed to them. A volume entitled *The Vision* was in his hand and he held it out as if it were a visiting-card. "I am a student," he said, "of the philosophical work of our chief poet. Does that entitle me to the company of others of the clan?"

"You present a good reference," said Anthony Wade. "My friend and myself are poets of another school. But we yield to none in our admiration of Yeats's later work, and we follow with interest his excursions into the realm of philosophy." Mortimer O'Looney, who was aware of only two philosophical terms, "subjective," and "objective," acquiesced in this statement. The stranger invited them to luncheon. "I am sure you will not decline," he said, "when I tell you that to-night I leave Ireland." "May we know the name of our entertainer?" Anthony Wade asked. "Gentlemen," the stranger said, "I am an Unknown. I know you both as poets and as men of wit and eloquence. I would have you with me as representatives of our country's illuminati. We need have no names."

The Unknown, as Anthony Wade afterwards said, had the build of a Guardsman in a romantic Victorian novel and there was something grave and passionate in his face. He spoke of Proust whom he had met in the salon of some Princess, and described him as being dressed like the hero of the *Sorrows of Satan.* He had offered his sword to d'Annunzio. He made Mortimer O'Looney and Anthony Wade feel that he placed them with the foremost Europeans. "I decline to know what angels I am entertaining," he said. The three talked well, and they made a leisurely session of the luncheon.

The day was declining; O'Looney had not forgotten that he had business to transact. He accepted the liqueur, but intimated that he could stay only a little while longer. "I hoped to have the privilege of hearing an unpublished poem," the Unknown said.

"We hoped to hear something of your own."

"I appreciate. I cannot create."

"After my friend, then," said Mortimer O'Looney.

There was a stage at which Anthony Wade became at once ultramontane and profane, when he would say, "I am a Catholic, but a pre-counter-reformation Catholic. To Hell with the Jesuits!" He reached that stage with the liqueurs. The only European figure whom he regretted having missed seeing was Leo XIII; he was, however, before the time he could have made the pilgrimage to him; he would have gone to him, not as the successor of St. Peter, but as to the last of the Latin poets. He repeated with exaltation Leo's verse, and the Unknown was able to remember and repeat the great invocation of St. Michael. His own best poetry, Anthony Wade said, was in Latin, the only language in which a poet could be Catholic, and he instanced Baudelaire and Lionel Johnson. Then he repeated his most recent ode. The Unknown appreciated the Latinity and talked charmingly and interestingly about the poem, lines of which he was able to remember. Then he turned to Mortimer O'Looney. O'Looney repeated his; his two listeners were moved by it.

"I shall remember this afternoon when I am under different stars," the Unknown said. "Men of my blood have been Spanish viceroys and Austrian field-marshals. I am the first of my house to take service with the British. Forgive my egotism if I count this as one of the disasters of the War."

The three went out together. O'Looney accepted a lift in their host's car. He had it stop before the neglected building in which the United Cemeteries had their office. The Unknown, taking farewell of him, presented him with a copy of Savage Landor's *Imaginary Conversations* elaborately bound. Then the car went on, Anthony Wade remaining with their host.

A flight of stairs, broad, bare and uncompromising, was before Mortimer O'Looney. He mounted them and came to a door over the dusty fanlight of which "United Cemeteries" was inscribed. He knocked and waited but no response came. He knocked again, and there was no stir within. "They make a mistake in closing so early—it's not good business," said Mortimer. He went down the stairs and into the street.

Then towards the quays. There was nothing interesting on the book-carts. He went and had tea. As he read one of the *Imaginary Conversations* he discovered in it a usable word—a word that could take the place of one in the poem: it could give the poem its title, too.

In the quiet light of the evening he went for a walk in the Park. The broom was in blossom, and before him was the gentle line of the Dublin hills. He had no reason to envy the lovers whom he passed. He was alone with his Genius. Lines of another poem, an unfinished one, came back into his memory. Before he knew that he was doing it, he had improved a line and was going on to finish the poem that he had left unfinished for three years. "To mouth that cold-faced wanton"—how much better that was than "to kiss that cold-faced wanton." The phrase was Shakespearean now. Here was the end: going to the window he sees the blue coming into the night. The rain on the windowpanes is like the tears on the face of the old hired musician who has been playing for the dance—"The old gray player." Better still, "tears on old failure's face." Outside the trees stand up, the branches wave. The world is as young as that in which Fionn hunted and Ulysses launched his ships. Mortimer O'Looney went on composing and re-composing his stanzas. The poem was finished, and he turned towards home.

He had had some good phrases in the original version, he knew. He saw the stanzas as he had drafted them and knew the sort of sheet they were on. A letter. A long, broad sheet. It was from the United Cemeteries Office. He remembered beginning the poem under the stamped signature. And the letter was six lines and it begged to inform him that the association was dissolved and that no further claims upon it could be liquidated.

He was near home. At the corner of the avenue there were two dead poplars; the bark was peeled off one, and the other tree had lumps that were like warts on its dead bark. These trees intruded themselves into his consciousness. Powerlessness, sadness, came over him again. Katie would open the door for him, and he would tell her that the purchase of the belt had been postponed. She had thought she would be wearing it to-morrow, the belt with the big clasps. "Thou hast hung the world upon nothing," Mortimer O'Looney said aloud, repeating the one line of the Koran that he knew.

THREE MEN

H E PRESENTED CARDS on which under his name, was the inscription, "Secretary and Founder of the Eblana Literary Society." Professionally he was a photographer: in outdoor seasons he went to castles that were visited by sightseers, demesnes that were open to the public, and sylvan places that people made trips to, and photographed groups and couples; in the winter he went to schools and photographed pupils in their classes—especially in First Communion and Confirmation classes; incidentally he had a photographing business in the town, but citizens who called at his premises usually found him taking tea after having come back from an expedition, or taking tea preparatory to going on one. He was a stocky man with a bush of hair and beard and eyes that glinted and glanced behind spectacles.

He called on Anthony Tisdil. Taking the card offered him, Anthony Tisdil read:

HOWARD TODD-GRUBB
SECRETARY AND FOUNDER OF
THE EBLANA LITERARY SOCIETY

Anthony Tisdil rubbed his forehead. These two fellow townsmen who had never before met socially talked about generalities.

Anthony Tisdil was discovered in the sitting-room of the house in which he lodged. Howard Todd-Grubb's glinting eyes took in the features of the sitting-room. On the walls were four coloured photographs representing idyllic scenes. On a table was a book with impressive covers—*Gladstone and His Contemporaries* was its title: the physiognomies of the statesmen who were contemporaries were often looked at by visitors, especially that of Daniel O'Connell with his hand within his vest. On the sideboard within a glass case was an owl: he had ruffled feathers and glazed eyes—a bird of night indeed. In the grate were pleated coloured papers. The chairs were plush-covered. There was also a horsehair sofa: on the edge of this Anthony Tisdil had been sitting.

The reason for his being in the sittingroom and the reason for his being called upon by Howard Todd-Grubb were connected. Anthony Tisdil had been in a railway collision the day before. He had come out of it unscathed. But his superiors in the office had given him a few days' leave of absence, and his landlady, out of sympathy with one who had undergone such an ordeal, and in recognition of the importance he had attained through it, had invited him (for the second time in his residence of twenty years) to occupy the sitting-room. His name had appeared in the account of the collision that was given in this morning's papers, and the Secretary and Founder of the Eblana Literary Society was calling upon him as upon an important, an exceptional man. Anthony Tisdil was about fifty: he was a little man with hair plastered across a bald streak on the crown of his head, with a scrubby moustache, a round face, and slightly protuberant eyes. He wore a brown coat which curved around his hips, black trousers, and very good elastic boots.

"Mr. Todd-Grubb," he said.

"The Eblana Literary Society," said Howard Todd-Grubb.

Anthony Tisdil rubbed his hand across his forehead. He had an inclination towards doing this when he was disturbed or bewildered.

"I have called to ask you to be one of our audience to-night," said the Secretary and Founder of the Eblana Literary Society. "You are now a man of mark in our town. I congratulate you on your miraculous escape."

Anthony Tisdil coughed and prepared to tell him about this escape, but found he had not the complete attention of his visitor. "Our distinguished—our very distinguished fellow-townsman, Loftus Mongan, is going to let us have the privilege of hearing an address from him to-night," he said. His hands were on the back of a chair; he leaned across and addressed Anthony Tisdil, who had again seated himself on the edge of the sofa. "I have no hesitation in saying it will be epoch-making. It will embody his reflections on the future of our country—his lifetime's reflections, I may say. He will deliver it himself—Loftus Mongan in person, Mr. Tisdil. Naturally I think this is a great event for the Society of which I am Secretary and Founder. You have never been to one of our meetings?"

Anthony Tisdil admitted that he had not.

"Then come, Mr. Tisdil," said Howard Todd-Grubb warmly. "This is a special invitation, and for a special occasion."

Anthony Tisdil stooped down to pick something off the floor. The veins on his forehead were noticeable. He murmured something that seemed to be in the nature of an assent. Howard Todd-Grubb took his hand, shook it heartily, and then let himself out of the room.

At the same hour Loftus Mongan, M.A., had entered the shop of H. MacCabe, Provision Merchant. A heavy walking stick was held firmly in his hand, a shabby overcoat was on his short, broad figure, and he wore a silk hat with a well-worn brim. He carried exercise-books in his hand and held a bag which bulged with some learned material. Holding stick and bag and books he spoke to H. MacCabe in a distinct voice and with clear enunciation, the voice of an educated man who was well used to delivering himself. Loftus Mongan said:

"This is the first afternoon I have been out of my rooms, and I rejoice in this salubrious weather. My studies kept me confined, but I have hope that I shall be able to go forth like a lion refreshed—or, rather I should say, like a giant refreshed—we must keep to the exact quotation, Mr. MacCabe. When our respected young townsman who is now the Treasurer of the State of Maryland used to come to me for lessons, I always impressed upon him the necessity for exactness of statement. I had a letter from him the other day, and he assured me that it was that exactness more than anything else that enabled him to rise to his present exalted position. I must say that with a position such as he has attained to in the New World he is a credit to all of us. A namesake of yours, too, Mr. MacCabe. Well, and did you read to-day's journals yet? My opinion is that the government means to break with us, Mr. MacCabe."

Thereupon Loftus Mongan delivered himself on a political topic. He was listened to respectfully, for he was a learned man and a Protestant Nationalist. Then he sank his resonant voice to a low but clear whisper:

"What is the smallest quantity of lard you sell?"

"A pennyworth."

"I shall trouble you for a pennyworth then. I have fish for dinner to-day, and my housekeeper will only cook them with lard." H. MaCabe put some lard upon a scale.

He had tubs of lard, slabs of butter, lumps and humps and hunks of cheese, barrels of pigs' heads, hams, gams, crubeens, flitches of bacon, sausages, white puddings, black puddings, pork-steaks, kidneys, tumbled rashers, and fatty ends of flitches of bacon. Although he had written over his shop "direct wine and spirit importer," and "licensed for consumption on the premises," H. MacCabe remained the Provision Merchant. He was never more himself than when he was slashing bacon with a huge and greasy blade. His wrapper was always greasy and always bore traces of his breakfast egg. His cheeks had the whiteness of sides of bacon, and his hands looked like meats that had not been thoroughly cured. He was a big, active, red-headed man, and one might wonder what enthusiasm or devotion kept him behind a counter in a space as wide as a railway carriage. Up and down this corridor he moved, wrapping up quarter pounds of butter and half pounds of rashers, and slicing bacon with his remarkable knife. He hummed as he made his adroit cuts.

"These ends of bacon now—I remember I purchased some before, and my housekeeper found them of use. Would you put up—well, less than half a pound—for me?"

The Merchant put up three rashers and the pennyworth of lard for Loftus Mongan, M.A. One rasher was fat, one extremely lean, and the other looked as if it had been in pickle.

"Is that all, Mr. Mongan?"

"I have been told to make a trial of one of your penny squares of bread. Please give it to me somewhat stale. And how much does it all come to?"

"Four pence! Dear me, what a lot can be got for money nowadays! You provision-dealers can be making very little."

"Nothing at all, Mr. Mongan—nothing at all, sir."

"What would you say to a measure of protection for this country?"

"I favour it because I understand that the Danes intend to give us no quarter." H. MacCabe spoke of the Danes, not as actual commercial competitors, but as vague and powerful oppressors. For him the nobles of Denmark still dowered their daughters with lands in Ireland.

Loftus Mongan put the rashers, the lard, and the bread into the bag he carried. It had been empty. Then with his stick placed under his arm, the bag and the exercise-books in his hand, he faced the provision dealer, the eyes under his shaggy brows confident again.

"More than one letter on the subject of free trade and protection has appeared in the public press over the signature of Loftus Mongan, M.A." he said.

"I know that, Mr. Mongan," said the Merchant.

"It is one of the subjects in which I take a great interest."

"I wish they were all as knowledgeable as yourself, Mr. Mongan."

"I have hardly any hopes of knowledge being cultivated in this part of the country—no hopes at all, I may say, Mr. MacCabe." He sank his voice to a whisper again. "How much do you think I am charging for lessons—English composition, arithmetic, Latin—two evenings a week?"

The Merchant leaned forward with interest now that commercial relations were the topic. "Tell me, Mr. Mongan," he said.

"Two shillings and sixpence—a bare half-crown. And how many pupils do you suppose I'm getting at that?"

"I couldn't say."

"Well, it doesn't matter. But if I did not have other means, my income would be small. I may tell you, Mr. MacCabe, that I am willing to take pupils of all ages. The man whose education has been neglected will be as sympathetically trained by me as the youth who has just entered a seminary. And pupils of the humblest social grade will be received. In my rooms." He laid his stick across the counter and looked into the Merchant's face. "I should be obliged if you would mention it, Mr. Mac-Cabe. Many think that I only give instruction to bank clerks and constabulary-men going up for promotion. But I should be glad to teach the rudiments to anyone—for the sake of our town, you know. Those whose education has been neglected and those of a lower social grade will be sympathetically in-structed by me. Good-bye to you." He took up his stick and strode out of the shop. His walk was quick and he swung his stick as he went along.

He marched past where Anthony Tisdil, still in the sitting-room, was perusing and re-perusing a page in a journal. He had propped it against the covers of *Gladstone and His Contem-poraries,* and, seated under the ruffled owl, was taking in sen-tences, was pondering on them. A man could always make some assertion of his will—that was the matter of the argu-ment that so weighed with him. He read about clerks in an

office. Their actions became part of routine, and it soon happened that they came to have as little power of assertion as
horses have. But, generally speaking, every day, and indeed
every portion of the day, a man had a chance of asserting his
will. At this moment his landlady's sister brought tea in. He
drank two cups, eating a slice of toast and a slice of bread and
butter. Then he perceived that his action was part of routine
and had nothing to do with his will. Did he or did he not want
tea at the moment? He could not tell. He always drank tea at
this hour on a Saturday when he was at home, taking two cups
with a slice of toast and a slice of bread and butter. But now he
began to be afraid that his action was part of routine. However,
he finished his tea.

Re-perusing the page, it was borne in on him that the first
effort towards its restoration was in the assertion of the will:
one might begin upon small affairs—compel oneself to write a
postcard, or restrain oneself from reading a newspaper in the
train. From that one should go on to deal with larger issues. . . .
But what stuck in Anthony Tisdil's mind and gave him matter
to ponder on was the comparison between a man and a horse.
A man could assert his will, a horse could not. In the beginning, as a young colt, the horse did assert his will, but after a
while he was broken of the habit, and his action became what
was termed automatic. It soon became impossible for a horse
to assert his will at all.

He used to be treated with more respect by the fellows
and the juniors in the office. Was it because everything he did
was now part of routine that he was being treated with a lessened consideration? Other fellows weren't treated as he was
being treated, after all. The other day, for instance. He had
been working with his head bent, and had felt a pressure on
his back. A junior, hardly a year in the place, a North of Ireland
fellow named McConigal, had laid a paper on his back and was
making some notes on it. He was quite cool about his action;
he just said he hadn't seen any place on the desk, and he
wanted to enter a name for a football team. But McConigal

wouldn't be so cheeky with any of the other fellows—he knew that now. Well, when he went back to the office he would assert his will on McConigal and the likes of him.

That morning Anthony Tisdil had wakened up at the regular hour. Then he realized that he did not have to go to the office, and he was pleased to think that he did not have to make a scramble to get the train and that the day was his own. He read an account of the collision in the papers and he saw his own name there—he was referred to as "Mr. Anthony Tisdil." When he went down to the railway-station people looked at him with curiosity and interest. This unusual day had prepared him to be interested in the question that the journal had given a page to. Usually Anthony Tisdil paid no attention at all to what he happened to read. But not having his habitual work before him, and seated in the unfamiliar surrounding of Mrs. Brophy's sitting-room, what was said in the article became real to him, like the voice of Burtt, his immediate superior.

His landlady's sister came into the room. She wanted to know would Mr. Tisdil go down and play a game of draughts with Mr. Brophy.

Anthony Tisdil rose to go. Then he realized that playing that game of draughts would be automatic action; he had been playing draughts with George Brophy every evening for some months. "Tell Mr. Brophy I'm not playing to-night," he said. "But he has the board all ready, Mr. Tisdil." Anthony hesitated. Then he said, "No, I can't go down. I've—I've a place that I have to go to to-night." It was then, after his landlady's sister had left the room, that he decided to go to the meeting of the Eblana Literary Society. He had no desire to hear Loftus Mongan and no interest in the future of the country or anything of the kind. But he was going to do something that would break the routine of his evenings. He took up *Gladstone and His Contemporaries*, deciding that he would read through the pages until the time came for him to go to the meeting of the Eblana Literary Society.

The click of billiard-balls could be heard from the more

frequented room below when the door of the Eblana Literary Society's premises was left open. It was open for a while after Anthony Tisdil had come in. There were three other arrivals: two young men who were at a table on which was a lighted lamp, and a man who was seated at the far end of the room, on the end of a bench. The Secretary and Founder of the Eblana Literary Society had not yet appeared.

Anthony Tisdil recognized the two young men: they were Daniel Meeney and Ignatius Greally. They were playing a game of cards. Daniel Meeney played as if he thought it was the grandest thing in the world to be able to oblige Ignatius Greally with that particular card. He rubbed his hands, not as Anthony Tisdil rubbed them, but by way of subdued applause. His hair was brushed back from his forehead; his features were distinct and good. Such features, lighted up with such decorous enthusiasm, were to be seen in the local church on the tinted statue of Saint Michael. He finished the game and stood up from the table.

"That was a nice game, Mr. Greally," he said (there was just a suspicion he said "dat").

The figure seated on the end of a bench at the back of the room was that of a blind man. "Will Mr. Loftus Mongan be here?" he asked, when Anthony seated himself in the middle of the bench above his.

Anthony Tisdil said that he understood that Loftus Mongan would very shortly arrive.

"He's a grand man, Mr. Loftus Mongan," said the blind man. "He made a speech last year and it was the best I ever listened to. I skipped in here because Mr. Mongan himself told me that he was going to make another speech to-night. He's a grand man, and very simple with the poor people, I must say." The blind man wore an ancient ulster with huge capes to it and a wide-brimmed hat. He could be very bitter to those who treated him as a beggar, but, as a matter of fact, he received charitable contributions from the well-do-do in the town. He was recommended to them on account of his piety. But the same blind man never made any attempts to conceal his ill-temper and his ill-will. Now he knocked on the floor with his stick. "I'm a long time here," he said.

It was then that Howard Todd-Grubb came amongst them. Anxious to be rid of the cares of office for the evening so that he might be free to devote all of his attention to Loftus Mongan's address, he appointed Daniel Meeney secretary pro tem. He welcomed Anthony Tisdil to the Eblana Literary Society, and introduced the two young men to him. Then he and the secretary pro tem. arranged the table for the speaker's convenience. "The proceedings will begin soon," the secretary pro tem. announced.

"I'm a long time here," said the blind man.

The secretary pro tem. assured him that he would not have long now to wait.

"Of course, I'm only a member of the public," said the blind man assertively, "but I came here to hear Mr. Loftus Mongan—why not, to be sure?"

Howard Todd-Grubb now lighted candles: he placed one on the table at the other side of the lamp, and two on the mantelpiece over the big empty grate. The blind man, feeling that illumination, perhaps, said "I suppose this is Mr. Loftus Mongan now."

But it was Lowry Muldoon who entered. His stiff black hair was upright, and his black eyes were jumping in his head at the sensation he was about to create.

"Did you see my miracle?" he cried. "God! Did any of you see my miracle?"

"What's the miracle, Lowry?" asked Ignatius Greally.

Lowry Muldoon stuck his hands in the pockets of an old Norfolk jacket that he wore, and swaggered across the room. "Give me a cigarette, somebody," he said. "The best miracle that ever was known in Ireland. The stigmata, you know. In all Irish papers. In the French papers, too, I believe. I invented it."

He puffed at the cigarette he had lighted at a candle, and swaggered around the room in high delight with himself. Invented the local miracle! Yes, Lowry Muldoon had invented it. There was no Maggie Halloran, although everyone in the district was convinced that the child was a neighbour of theirs. Wishing to have the local journal quoted in the Dublin dailies Muldoon had written an account of an imaginary miracle with startling headlines above it. The announcement that he now made was a shock to all in the room of the Eblana Literary Society.

The blind man muttered his disapprobation.

"You'll get sacked off your paper for this," said Ignatius Greally.

"Indeed, I won't. I'm running the paper myself. Hempson has been drinking since Christmas."

"Will you read anything to us to-night, Mr. Muldoon?" asked the secretary pro tem.

Howard Todd-Grubb, who was standing at the door and looking down the stairway, intervened. "We have reserved the evening for a discussion of the address that Loftus Mongan is going to deliver," he declared.

But Lowry Muldoon had already taken a paper out of the inside pocket of his coat. "I have something with me. I don't know if it will do. Listen to this . . ."

"The proceedings will not begin until Loftus Mongan . . ."

But Lowry Muldoon had taken a place at the table, holding the pages of his manuscript in his hand. A grey-haired young man with a remarkably smooth face came in just then. He stood near the door. Folding his arms, he took the attitude of a listener. This attitude imposed on the others, all except the blind man, the mood of an audience. Lowry Muldoon began:

"Every smoker has had experience of the last match. Not uncommmonly it is something like the following:—a windy road, a traveller remote from towns, a match-box almost empty, and a keen desire for tobacco. The traveller attempts his pipe, and lights match after match, and each in turn is blown out before he can use it. Soon comes the last match of all. This he nurses so tenderly that the wax or wood ignites thoroughly, and he lights his pipe. Overjoyed at his good fortune, he holds the flame to the fury of the wind, and still it burns steadily. He takes the pipe from his mouth and apostrophises the match. 'You little beast,' he says, 'you'll burn now, will you, when I don't want you any longer? Then burn you shall, right to the end!' Thus holding it at arm's length he watches it burn. It shortens and shortens. At length he drops it upon the ground where it flickers for a moment or two, and expires. Then, he puts his pipe into his mouth again, and lo! it is out."

"Is there much more of it?" asked the secretary pro tem., Howard Todd-Grubb having again gone out to watch for the approach of Loftus Mongan.

"Eight pages," said Lowry Muldoon.

"It's all right, I think. You can read it when the discussion is over," said the obliging secretary pro tem.

"No arrangement can be made until we have Mr. Loftus Mongan amongst us," said Howard Todd-Grubb. "I think he is approaching." He went to the door.

But the person whom he ushered in a moment later was not Loftus Mongan. She was a spinster, middle-aged and energetic-looking, who had a piece of worn fur around her neck and a bright ribbon in her hat, and a long black rigid-seeming coat. She was Miss Sears, who kept the lodging-house in which Loftus Mongan stayed; she was the person he had in mind when he spoke of "my housekeeper." Miss Sears had come to inform the Society that Mr. Loftus Mongan could not be with them that night.

"Do I hear that he is not coming after all?" the blind man asked Anthony Tisdil.

Anthony Tisdil said that he understood that Mr. Loftus Mongan was unable to come.

"Dear, dear, dear! What brought me out at all to-night?" said the blind man.

Anthony Tisdil, noticing that Miss Sears had presented Howard Todd-Grubb with a roll of manuscript, told him that the society was going to have the paper read to them in any case.

"Oh, murther, it's himself we want to hear," said the blind man bitterly.

Loftus Mongan was ill and confined to bed. Speaking from a seat which she had taken, Miss Sears informed the Society that he had been taken ill with cramps in the stomach. He was in agony. She had wanted him to lie down, but nothing would do him but get the papers ready for the Literary Society's meeting. Up to the last minute he had intended to be present. But when she had heard him say that he had become dizzy, she had taken the papers out of his hands and had come along with them. Mr. Loftus Mongan had sent a message by her asking Mr. Todd-Grubb to get one of the gentlemen present to read his address. And, if they would permit her, she would remain while it was being read, and bring back a report of how it had been received.

The secretary pro tem. stated that a rule of the Society disallowed their having females present during their proceedings. Thereupon Howard Todd-Grubb proposed that the rule should be suspended, so that Miss Sears might remain during the reading of Loftus Mongan's paper. The proposal was agreed to, and Miss Sears, who had stood up during the short discussion upon the motion, seated herself on one of the back benches. Lowry Muldoon having gone out when the interest in his essay expired, there were present the secretary pro tem., Daniel Meeney, Ignatius Greally, Anthony Tisdil, the young grey-haired man with the smooth face, the blind man, Miss Sears, and, of course, Howard Todd-Grubb. The secretary and founder of the Eblana Literary Society stood with his elbow upon the mantelpiece, and in the light of the candles his glasses gleamed, heightening the expectancy that was in the room.

But at the moment when the conscientious secretary pro tem. was picking open the tape that was around the roll of manuscript, another member entered the room. He was

Charles Hempson, the editor of the local paper in which the first account of the imaginary miracle had been given. He was purple-nosed, and wore a soiled white waistcoat. He left the door open, and the knocking and clicking of billiard-balls was very audible as Daniel Meeney pronounced the title of Loftus Mongan's paper: "Citizenship in the Future State."

In less than ten minutes after this title had been pronounced, Anthony Tisdil, Ignatius Greally, and the blind man, after an initial, momentary eagerness, had fallen into a gloomy stupor. Miss Sears remained upright and impassive in attitude and manner. Charles Hempson, tilting his chair back as he sat in it, squeezed his head in his hand from time to time in a significant and ostentatious manner. But the grey-haired young man manifested complete approval of what was being read. And Howard Todd-Grubb, seated near the reader, nodded his head, his spectacle glinting in a remarkable manner.

Why Howard Todd-Grubb did not himself undertake the reading of the address on Citizenship in the Future State will remain a mystery. But it was evident that his unfamiliarity with Loftus Mongan's caligraphy made the secretary pro tem. read the manuscript haltingly. After a ten minutes' reading he began to show dismay at the number of pages that were still in his hand, and time and time again he gave the impression that, in his judgment, he was dealing with an undiminishable quantity. It was evident that not Idea, but Number, was his preoccupation. A time came when he had to be prompted by Howard Todd-Grubb, who took a place beside him and even read over the reader's shoulder. Then there were two voices delivering passages from the manuscript and occasionally giving divergent readings. As read by the secretary pro tem. with the assistance of the secretary and founder of the Eblana Literary Society, the address was undeniably long. Pythagoras, Berkeley, and Burke were the philosophers quoted in it.

At last Daniel Meeney laid the last page on the back-turned pages before him as Howard Todd-Grubb, wiping his spectacles, looked expectantly at the audience before him.

"I think we may say that the Eblana Literary Society thanks Mr. Loftus Mongan," he said, as Miss Sears came to take the manuscript off the table.

"In my opinion," said the young man with the grey hair, "we have listened to a very remarkable—a very profound work."

"In what way remarkable?" Charles Hempson interjected.

"In its general conception, first of all," said the grey-haired young man.

"Excuse me," said Charles Hempson, "but you know nothing about conceptions, general or otherwise."

It was evident that Charles Hempson had more to say, but he waited. He now sat with the chair turned around, his arms leaning on the back of it. He held the attention of the society.

"I have told this young man in effect that he is no better than a fool," he said. "He is a fool because he speaks on a subject he knows nothing about."

"Mr. Meeney," said the young man, "I ask are Mr. Hempson's remarks in order?"

"In order? No, I think not. He. Hempson, I'll have to remind you that you are not in order."

"There was one passage that I seemed to get a glimmering of an idea out of," said Charles Hempson deliberately, "and that was a passage on the last two pages of that magnitudinous manuscript. May I ask the secretary to read us that passage once more?"

All present, even the fatigued secretary pro tem., were now stirred up and eager. Howard Todd-Grubb snatched up the manuscript which Miss Sears had not yet taken into her possession, and gave a clear and ringing delivery to the last pages of the manuscript. These passages were by way of peroration; they had little—in fact they had nothing to do with the general idea of the paper which, some pages before, had been rounded off and completed. Loftus Mongan had wanted to convey a sense of a coming dawn in the country: he had written those passages that very morning; it had happened that his sleep had been broken, and he had been actually present at the phenomenon described.

"Is it not the fable of the poets," Howard Todd-Grubb read, "that birds sing at a certain hour in a way that is different from their song at other times? That hour is long before light. You hear the voice of one bird and then the voices of the choir. You rise and draw back your curtains. The stars are apparent in the sky, and the wind of night is above the voices of the birds; the dog, unaware that his watch is near over, barks. And still goes up that murmurous song. One bird sings disinguishably. But the song that goes up is like the sound of the leaves of the forest, or the falling of raindrops, or the hum of bees. It is as if all the birds were in one nest and, with necks raised and dewy wings spread out, were singing, or rather, were murmuring a song. It is as if the birds consecreated to this light the beginnings out of which have come their several songs. The murmur goes on and on, the star is in the sky, the dog barks, the gas-lamps of the country-town gleam. It gets brighter. The wind has no longer the wail of the night. The dog is satisfied with the honesty of the day and ceases to bark. The geese waken up and cackle. The morning song of the birds now ceases. And so it is with us who are here. The wail of the wind is around us; the voices of dogs and geese are the only ones that are heeded. But we shall give forth a melody again. And amongst us there will be one clear voice that shall be heeded."

Howard Todd-Grubb read these lines with fervour, declaiming them a little, but without any gesture. At one side of him stood Miss Sears, at the other, Daniel Meeney: she looked like a landlady who has supplied a reckoning and who knows that not one jot nor tittle can be taken from it; he looked like a man who had been aroused from listlessness, but who was about to sink back into listlessness again. Ignatius Greally, Anthony Tisdil, and the blind man were attentive. The young grey-haired man made no manifestation, but it was plain from his expression that nothing need have been added to the effect that had been produced. But Charles Hempson, his chair tilted back, his thumbs stuck in the arm-holes of his soiled white waistcoat, looked as insolent as before.

"Fine—very fine!" said the grey-haired young man.

"Fine—very fine, indeed!" said Charles Hempson. "Our friend has described the feelings of a man wakening up after hitting the booze for a fortnight. I think some of us know the state described. But I shall say to the gentleman who has perpetrated the work, 'I don't think we can do anything for you, sir.'"

Howard Todd-Grubb lost control of himself. "I think I speak on behalf of the decent members of this society," he said, "and I speak as founder and secretary of it, and speaking as founder and secretary and on behalf of the decent members, I say that we will not be able to tolerate Mr. Hempson's presence at any more of our meetings."

"The members of the society are invited to make a criticism of works put before them," said Charles Hempson. "Am I to understand that when the Society says criticism, it means fulsome adulation?"

"No, sir," said the founder and secretary of the Eblana Literary Society.

"Mr. Hempson!" said Miss Sears reprovingly.

Mr. Hempson addressed the secretary pro tem. "May I draw your attention to the fact that there are females present during the proceedings," he said.

"The rule was suspended to permit Miss Sears to be present during the reading of Loftus Mongan's paper," said Daniel Meeney.

"But not to join in the debate, I presume."

"No, not to join in the debate," said Daniel Meeney.

"Very well. Then I hope I shall be permitted to continue."

All the time Charles Hempson had been speaking, the blind man had been tapping the floor with his stick and clicking his tongue by way of protest. "Is there to be nothing but argufying?" he kept saying. "Why didn't Mr. Loftus Mongan come in?"

"Mr. Loftus Mongan shouldn't demean himself by coming to such a place," Miss Sears said, oblivious of the fact that speech was debarred her in that assembly.

"I'm only a member of the public," said the blind man, "but I want to tell you that Mr. Hempson is always making trouble. Didn't I hear him at a Board of Guardians' Meeting last year? He was that overbearing while they were reading Mr. Loftus Mongan's oration that I couldn't make out at all what it was about."

"Neither could your betters, my good man," said Charles Hempson.

"Mr. Hempson," said Miss Sears, "this poor man may have come to misfortune, but he is a well educated man—anybody can see that."

"Leave him alone—leave him alone," said the blind man. "But I'll tell you this—the Society will have no respect in this town as long as no member will put a hand on that man to turn him out."

"To turn me out?" exclaimed Charles Hempson, standing up from the chair.

"Is there no one here who will rid the Society, who will rid Loftus Mongan of this mocker?" Howard Todd-Grubb exclaimed. "I cannot deal with him on account of my glasses."

Anthony Tisdil rose up. In Howard Todd-Grubb's voice there was appeal, and appeal had not been made to him for many a long day. Perhaps his intention was merely to place himself at the side of the Secretary and Founder of the Eblana Literary Society and give him the support of a man who had been in a railway collision. As soon as he stood up, "Sit down, my man," said Charles Hempson to him.

Then Anthony Tisdil went towards him. The grey-haired young man had opened the door, perhaps with the intention of inducing the editor to make an exit. Anthony Tisdil pitched himself upon Charles Hempson. Now the editor was not steady on his legs (he had been leaning on the back of a chair) and the impact of Anthony's body made him lurch towards the door. At the threshold there was a struggle. Making an effort Anthony Tisdil thrust his man out. He plucked himself from

Hempson's clawing hands and got back into the room. The grey-haired young man shut fast the door.

"Open the door! Damn you, open the door for me," came from the man outside.

All the occupants of the room except the blind man stood before the door. "The door will not open to you, Charles Hempson, mocker," Howard Todd-Grubb declared. There was a rattling at the door; a call from downstairs was heard; Charles Hempson's steps were listened to as they descended the stairway. But still Miss Sears remained on guard at the door.

"I move that the best thanks of the Eblana Literary Society be returned to our distinguished and courageous guest for his effort in combating the ferocious opposition to Loftus Mongan's address, and that the Society inform Loftus Mongan of that effort." It was Howard Todd-Grubb made the motion. It was seconded by the secretary pro tem. and supported by the grey-haired young man (it was disclosed that his name was Peter-Paul Duffy). The blind man said, "Hear Hear!" tapping the floor with his stick. As for Anthony Tisdil, he was overcome by the effort he had made. He sank into the chair at the table. Ignatius Greally emptied a glass of water on his head. He sat there, his head bent mechanically, wiping the back of his neck where the water was dampening his collar.

"Hush," said Miss Sears at the doorway, "somebody is coming up the stairs. I firmly believe that it is Mr. Mongan himself."

"Is Mr. Mongan coming himself?" asked the blind man hopefully.

And when Miss Sears opened the door Loftus Mongan was actually there. He entered, massive with his thick-set figure, his silk hat, his walking-stick. He looked like a man who had been replenished. In a minute his hat and overcoat were off and his stick was laid in a corner. He took no account of the statement that his paper had been read by the secretary pro tem. He unrolled the manuscript he had taken out of Miss Sear's hands, and began his address.

His voice was resonant, although now and again there

was a croak of hoarseness in it. As he went on Ignatius Greally
looked at Daniel Meeney as if he were thunderstruck to think
that the reading of an address could convey so little of its
substance and spirit. The secretary pro tem., picking up the
pages as they swept out of the hand of the reader, read them
with startled interest. Peter-Paul Duffy was rapt by it all; occasionally he wrote a note on his shirt-cuff. Howard Todd-Grubb
preserved his equanimity; it was as he had divined through
Daniel Meeney's reading; he nodded from time to time to mark
his acceptance of salient passages. The difference between the
address as read by the secretary pro tem. and as delivered by
the author was the difference between despondency and flash-
ing hope. The blind man's face was lighted up as if he looked
on the sun again. As for Anthony Tisdil he was caught and
held by a title that Loftus Mongan introduced early into his
address and frequently made use of—"The Illuminati." All that
was to be achieved was to be achieved through the Illuminati.
And the Illuminati were those present who were sharing in the
thoughts that were being delivered by Loftus Mongan. Miss
Sears was not visibly moved; she sat on a bench at the door,
her hands in her lap, her eyes closed tightly.

   With the first words of Loftus Mongan's address something had come near—so near that the opening of the door
might bring it amongst men. That something was a future in
which life was ennobled. Dignity and high reward adhered to
every labour. Everyone had influence in creating a state that
was great and respected. Loftus Mongan's belief in his fellow-
men—especially in such of them as surrounded him at the
moment—banished disbelief and distrust. The Illuminati were
those present. Anthony Tisdil, by virtue of being there, was
one of the Illuminati. After the peroration about the birds singing in the dawn there were words spoken to the Illuminati
directly. They were as a call to them. Loftus Mongan laid the
papers on the table and walked up and down the room.

   He inquired about the reception that his address had had
on its first reading. He heard about Charles Hempson's mocks

and gibes. Then he heard about Anthony Tisdil's heroic inter-
vention. Anthony was made known to him. He took Anthony's hand.

Lowry Muldoon burst in. "Somebody give me a
cigarette," he said. It was felt by members present that he was
an emissary of the enemy, and his reception was a guarded
one. Ignatius Greally tendered him the cigarette; he lit it at an
expiring candle and paced about the room. People were leaving the billiard-room below.

"Where is Charles Hempson?" Loftus Mongan asked.

"In the billiard-room, snoring drunk," said Lowry Muldoon. "Give me your manuscript," he said. "I'll put it in the
Standard this week. I'll write the headings for it myself."

"I have something better to do with my manuscript, sir,"
said Loftus Mongan.

"It is the best offer I can make," said Lowry Muldoon.
The lamp on the table flickered and went out. A candle went
out. Lowry Muldoon tried to re-light his cigarette, and snuffed
out another candle. Exits began. Miss Sears took the hand of
the blind man and led him down the stairway. Peter-Paul
Duffy bade a respectful good-night to Loftus Mongan and
went out. Lowry Muldoon took Ignatius Greally and Daniel
Meeney by the arms and pushed them along. "You'll have to
get me a pint," he said.

"Come, Mr. Tisdil, join us; be one of the Illuminati,"
Loftus Mongan said, as he took Anthony's arm. "What could I
say when I met the rest of them?" Anthony Tisdil asked.
"There are not so many of us as yet; in fact, there is only myself
and my friend, Howard Todd-Grubb. Take your place side by
side with us." "Oh, if there's only you and Mr. Todd-Grubb, I
wouldn't mind joining," said Anthony Tisdil. "It's fellows I'd
be afraid of." He thought of Burtt in the office. Burtt nor the
others would never know that he belonged to this wonderful
band of transformers. But it would be in his own mind, and
that would help him to stand up to Burtt and the others. "Give
me your hand; take Mr. Todd-Grubb's hand; we will join to-

gether on this bridge," said Loftus Mongan. They stood on the bridge and the river flowed below them, and Anthony Tisdil thought of a line of poetry, "I stood on the bridge at midnight," and he was elevated by the thought that poetry was appropriate to the situation in which he was. "The Illuminati have come into existence," said Loftus Mongan. "The Illuminati have come into existence," exclaimed Howard Todd-Grubb fervently. The blind man's stick was heard tapping the pavement as he went towards wherever his domicile was. "Good luck to you, Mr. Mongan," he said as he heard a voice that he recognized. "It was grand, grand." Anthony Tisdil felt that he was one of three who had perceptible grandeur about them—The Illuminati.

SELECTED SHORT STORIES OF PADRAIC COLUM

was composed in 10-point Linotron 202 Palatino and leaded two points
by Coghill Book Typesetting Co.;
with display type in Folkwang and Erbar by J. M. Bundscho, Inc.;
printed by sheet-fed offset on 55-pound, acid-free Glatfelter Antique Cream,
adhesive bound with paper covers
by Maple-Vail Book Manufacturing Group, Inc.;
with paper covers printed in two colors
by Philips Offset Company, Inc.;
and published by

SYRACUSE UNIVERSITY PRESS
SYRACUSE, NEW YORK 13244-5160

Irish Studies

IRISH STUDIES presents a wide range of books interpreting important aspects of Irish life and culture to scholarly and general audiences. The richness and complexity of the Irish experience, past and present, deserves broad understanding and careful analysis. For this reason an important purpose of the series is to offer a forum to scholars interested in Ireland, its history, and culture. Irish literature is a special concern in the series, but works from the perspectives of the fine arts, history, and the social sciences are also welcome, as are studies which take multidisciplinary approaches.

Irish Studies is a continuing project of Syracuse University Press and is under the general editorship of Richard Fallis, associate professor of English at Syracuse University.

IRISH STUDIES, edited by Richard Fallis